Angela's Answer

BOOK ONE

Angel Light

Angela's Answer

⌐○ PAT MATUSZAK ○⌐

LIVING
INK
BOOKS
Writing Worth Reading™

An Imprint of AMG Publishers.

Angela's Answer
Copyright © 2008 by Pat Matuszak
Published by Living Ink Books, an imprint of AMG Publishers
6815 Shallowford Rd.
Chattanooga, Tennessee 37421

ISBN 978-089957875-0
First printing—April 2008
Cover designed by Left Coast Design, Portland, Oregon
Interior design and typesetting by Reider Publishing Services,
    West Hollywood, California
Edited and Proofread by Rebecca Miller, Dan Penwell, Rich Cairnes,
    and Rick Steele

Printed in the United States of America
14 13 12 11 10 09 08 –S– 7 6 5 4 3 2 1

This book is dedicated to my loving family,
who inspired it, and especially to my husband,
John, who encouraged me to write it.

Note to readers:

This book is a fictional story and is not meant to portray real people, places, or events. It is not written to be a theological guide, though it is the hope of the author that it might inspire readers to be guided by the One who is life's true Light.

Psalm 91:9-11

For more information on Angela and her adventures, and to find clues about what will happen next, go online to:

www.AngelClues.com

Contents

Acknowledgments

I'M SO THANKFUL for family and friends who supported my writing effort with prayer and for the grace and inspiration of the One who answers those requests.

Many thanks to those who gave wise and generous editorial advice, not the least of whom is Dan Penwell, whose subtle expertise with both the pen and the golf club should be praised.

Thanks to Trevor Overcash and Left Coast Design for crafting a wonderful cover, to Dale Anderson for championing the series to the industry, and to Rich Cairnes and the rest of AMG's editorial team for their skillful help and patience.

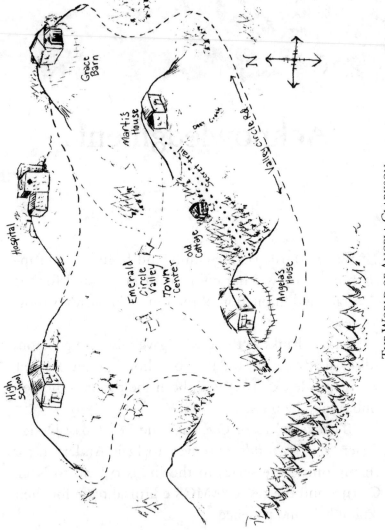

The World of Angela Clarkson

The First Mistake

ANY ARTIST would have loved to paint or photograph the scene. A slender girl with dark flowing hair rode a golden horse across a green hill into the setting sun. However, if a photographer had a zoom lens, he'd wonder why the girl wasn't enjoying the ride. Why was she frowning, shaking her head, and talking to herself? The person who was watching the girl didn't have a camera, though, and he didn't have to wonder what was bothering the girl. He knew. That's why he was watching and waiting.

She wasn't actually talking to herself; Angela was talking to her horse, who flicked back one golden ear, then the other, to listen to her. His silver mane rippled as his neck seemed almost to be nodding in agreement with his rider's complaints. "Well, that is about the last straw, Roy," Angela grumbled as she bounced along slouching in the saddle in a posture contrary to the one her riding instructors had drilled into her. Good form just didn't matter today. Who cared what kind of form she used now, anyway? Her last good riding partner was turning in her saddle and selling one of the best cross-country ponies in the county to buy a car . . . of all things! A stupid, noisy car—probably to ride around with some stupid, noisy, new friends. And after all their promises to stay horsewomen together, after other girls their age left 4-H horse club one by one to spend their time and money at the mall, gawking and cackling with other lame, boy-crazy girls. It was sad. And Angela was sad. And she was mad at the same time.

2

Angela had ridden her horse, Roy Rogers, over to Marti's barn to go for their usual Saturday afternoon ride through the Metro Park trails. It was a great ride and took at least two hours to complete. She hadn't bothered to call because they'd talked about going at the last horse club meeting. They rode together almost every Saturday when it wasn't raining. Once school started in Northern Ohio, rain was frequent. But when it wasn't raining, the weather was perfect. Crisp, colorful, and fresh in a way that made up for the muggy, fly-infested summer. Angela and Roy rounded the bend and saw the familiar white clapboard barn, but the mustang pulled to a stop suddenly and snorted. There was a strange car at Marti's barn.

Angela noticed the car wasn't running, so she urged Roy forward. The sturdy mustang was very protective of his rider. He didn't like things that were out of the ordinary, so he moved ahead cautiously.

"Hey-y-y, Marti," Angela yelled and gave a loud whistle as she approached. It was like a secret handshake between them, and Marti's black Arabian pony, Bobcat, whinnied a greeting in reply.

The sound reassured Roy, and he trotted ahead eagerly, answering with a call about an octave deeper. Not only were the girls best friends, but their horses were, too. Bobcat was just a hand shorter than Roy, though he was a pony by official rules at most horse shows. His size put him on the borderline and that allowed him to enter classes designated "horses only" at certain shows. Marti still looked the perfect size riding him, even though the petite blond girl was about to turn sixteen.

Marti had tacked up Bobcat with saddle and bridle, but she wasn't in the saddle warming up to ride. Instead, she stood in the corral holding the reins and talking with a little girl and two adults who looked like parents. It wasn't unusual for Marti to give riding lessons to younger kids from the 4-H club, so Angela guessed that was what had been going on before she arrived.

Angela was wrong about that. It was her *first mistake* of the day, but it wouldn't be the last.

"Well, thanks so much, Marti," said the mom as she turned to go. "We'll call you later to make arrangements."

Marti mumbled goodbye as she looked sheepishly out of the corner of her eye at Angela.

"Hey, I brought Cokes and granola bars for the turn," Angela called, patting a lumpy saddlebag that hung over the utility rope she always had tied to the back of the saddle. "We'd better get going if we want to be back by dark.

That was the only rule their parents had for long rides; just be back to the barn by dark. They knew their moms would be watching from each of their houses for the barn lights to come on, a sign that their daughters reached home safe and sound. The cell phone reception in the park couldn't be counted on, but the girls always checked in at "the turn"—a riding center at the halfway point, located next to the county park system. They could use the pay phone there, and Sarah Grace, the center's director and the girls' riding teacher since second grade, kept an eye out for them. If they forgot to phone home, she'd remind them before they left.

Angela waited expectantly for her friend to answer, but Marti just stood there looking at her. She didn't swing up into Bobcat's saddle or anything. She just stood there with a funny expression on her face. Angela wondered if she was going to cry or something.

"Hey, what is it?" she finally asked and jumped down from Roy's back.

Marti dropped Bobcat's reins and grabbed her friend in a big, desperate hug. Then she did start crying. "I sold him," Marti managed to say between sobs. "I just sold Bobcat."

The Next Mistakes

WHAT DO YOU mean? Why? Why would you do that?"

Angela took Marti by both arms and looked into her tear-streaming eyes. Marti rubbed her face on one sleeve and managed to stop crying. She pulled off her black riding helmet and fluffed her spiky blond hair to fix the "hat-head" look the cap always caused. As she did, the whole story came pouring out.

"My parents—oh, I can't stand to say this out loud, but I might as well get used to it—my parents are getting a divorce."

"Oh, no," Angela said. She hugged her friend again. "You said they'd been arguing a lot, but I didn't realize it was that bad."

Marti choked back her tears enough to answer. "It's worse. Even though they've been a nightmare to live with, I thought there was still hope they'd work things out as long as they were here together. And I still had Bobcat. But yesterday they said they're going to sell the farm. They can't afford two houses, so they've found two separate condos to live in. But, get this, both places are out of the school district. I'm losing everything—my family, my home, my horse, and even my friends."

"What? That's terrible. And you won't even be able to go to our school anymore?"

"Well, I found out I can commute under some hardship rule if I arrange my own transportation," Marti explained. "So I'm doing it. I'm selling Bobcat so I can afford to buy a car when I turn sixteen next month."

"No!" Angela almost screamed. Roy Rogers jumped slightly to one side, startled.

"I have to. It's the only way. That little girl you saw is his new owner. She needs lessons, so I'll at least get to see him when I give them. They said I could ride him anytime I want. But they live across town, so you and I probably won't get to ride together anymore." It was too much. Marti broke down crying, and this time Angela did, too.

So there wasn't any trail ride. They untacked the horses and let them play in the corral. The girls sat on bales of straw and watched, drinking the Cokes and eating up the granola bars. They went inside and raided the fridge for more substantial food and looked at photos from the last

6

horse show they entered together. Eventually, Marti's mom came home and checked to see what they were up to. She seemed concerned, apologetic, and crushed. It didn't help things. Angela wanted to feel sorry for her—she knew that would be the right thing to do—but she couldn't. All her sympathies went to herself and her friend. When Mrs. Philips offered to let her leave Roy in the barn and drive her home, Angela was curt in her reply.

"No thanks. I wouldn't want to inconvenience you," she said, flinging a look that was supposed to be "withering" at her friend's mom. Angela wasn't that good at withering looks, but Mrs. Philips got the point.

"All right, but it's getting dark," she replied cautiously. "If you're going to ride, you'd better get going. I'll call your mom and let her know you are on your way."

So that was how Angela made her *second mistake* of the day.

"I'm so sorry about everything, Marti," she told her friend as they said goodbye at the corral. Marti looked like someone had wrung the life out of her; the expression on her face was hopeless. There was nothing more for Angela to do or say, so she rode off "into the sunset," as the saying goes. Alone.

Roy Rogers' hoofbeats were slow and sad, echoing down the deserted road. All that was missing was some sad harmonica music to top off the day. Angela slouched along, munching her dark thoughts about the mess that had been served up for her by fate or whatever. Now she d be the only high-school-age member left in the horse club, so there would be no one to talk to who'd understand her real life. Just little kids and their little ponies.

Angela and Marti had been the daring duo of the club, the first to try out new paths or to Google satellite photos to find an alternate way to get to a destination by horseback. They won their share of ribbons at fairs and shows, but what they really enjoyed was trail riding across the rolling hills of their suburban town.

They'd discovered one trail they kept completely to themselves, however, because they knew if their parents found out, it would surely be forbidden. They used it mainly when they were in a hurry to get home because it shaved at least five minutes off the trip between their houses.

8

The isolated path was just a deer trail now, and its beauty was wasted on wildlife except for the two adventuring riders. Willow branches, raspberry bushes, and wild grapevines encroached on the trail and in places they hung over the narrow track until they almost formed a tunnel. The end of one tunnel opened into a small clearing where there was an abandoned cottage. The path must have been a wider road to the cottage long ago when someone lived there, but the forest had reclaimed it over the years. The two girls shared the little cottage's secluded beauty only with deer and wild birds, and entertained each other by making up romantic stories about who might have lived there.

The Next Mistakes

The end of the trail that was near Marti's house began along the edge of some power lines that crested the ridge overlooking the new highway, then plunged down into a valley where there was an old homesteader cemetery with a dozen baroque headstones and a mausoleum with ornate statues carved into the doorway. After the cemetery, the path dropped into a deeper valley where a creek bubbled past the little abandoned cottage, then the path wound back up a steep hill and came out on Angela's street. The girls stopped at the cottage a couple of times that summer and sat on the tiny, sagging porch, eating raspberries as the horses munched grass on what looked like it might have been a front lawn. They wondered who had tended it long ago. The one-room house had no glass left in the windows and no front door. A wild rose vine climbed the wall and blossomed small pink buds most of the season.

As the sunlight rapidly slipped away, Angela decided to take the path so she could make curfew.

It was her *third mistake* of the day, but not yet her last.

○ 3

The Last Mistake

HORSES ARE famous for "smelling the barn" on their way home, and Roy Rogers was no exception. The mustang knew it was time for dinner—a nice crunchy carrot and a shelf of hay forked from the overflowing loft into his feed rack. He pranced and tossed his head, asking to speed up the trip, but Angela was careful not to let him plunge blindly ahead on the shadowy trail. The path was just a bit tricky in full daylight, with unexpected roots and chipmunk holes from lack of use, and the light at dusk made it even more difficult to gauge depth perfectly. She shifted her weight onto the back of her heels and saddle to let Roy know it was time to settle down.

"Who-o-o-a," she murmured soothingly. "Chill out, Roy. I'm not in the mood to argue with you now."

Roy snorted disapproval, but obeyed. As they came to the cemetery, Angela saw fog was settling into low spots as the temperature dropped for the night. Wispy shreds of gray swirled and circled, so they had to go carefully to make sure not to trip on any of the stone grave markers hidden by fog the same color as granite. Angela was glad they hadn't charged around the corner.

Marti had joked about ghosts, jumping Bobcat over some of the larger stone monuments, but Angela couldn't do it. Maybe she was frightened by the thought of a corpse under Roy's feet or maybe it was just the disrespect it showed for something, well, sacred. She didn't consider herself *religious*, but she did go to church on holidays, and she believed there was something greater than herself. Some power had created all this natural beauty.

"Maybe there's someone up there who watches over us," she told Marti, who teased her for not following her over the headstone jump. "If there is, I need all the help I can get. I don't want to make God, or whatever, mad at me if I can avoid it."

Now she thought about needing help with her problems. God was such a big concept. Did he really exist? If he did, was he in the business of helping ordinary, nonsaints with troubles like losing a best friend? If only there was a way to know for sure. What she thought she'd really like was a place to go to with a nice sign on the door like:

ANSWERS TO ALL QUESTIONS FOUND HERE.

If there was a God, why didn't he make himself known plainly? Why all this smoke and shadow around himself?

Roy interrupted her internal philosopher. He shied, skittering to one side of the path. An experienced horse-woman, Angela could tell the location of the thing that had scared him by the direction of his movement and the tilt of his head. She glanced that way while keeping her focus on calming her mount and preventing him from tripping. What she thought she saw, she knew she could not have seen. She blinked a couple of times at what looked like a human figure ahead. As she refocused, she realized it was just an oddly shaped tree. The movement she heard and briefly saw must have been a chipmunk racing up the trunk for safety. Strange. For that split second it looked like an eight-foot-tall man with a gray cape . . . or mothlike wings. Now it just looked like a tree, and Roy had calmed enough to go around it, though he skirted it at as great a distance as she would allow him.

"I'm sorry, buddy," Angela soothed. "We should have left sooner. We're almost home now. Hang on."

Ahead she could see the sun falling behind the roof of the old abandoned cottage. A golden glow filtered through its empty windows, making it look like there were lights on inside. If only it were her house and she were home already, she mused as she swallowed back a yawn. She was really becoming tired. Bed and a warm quilt would feel great after this chilly dampness.

But as she got closer to the cottage, her heart raced. She could clearly see that the sunset was not lighting the cottage. There were lights coming from inside the old place. Impossible, yet true. Someone was inside.

No one could possibly be living there. The place was just a shell and it certainly didn't have electricity for lights. Was it some criminal hiding from the police . . . or something even worse? They had never met anyone on their secret path before. Who else could have found it? Maybe she could just sneak by and not be heard.

The sound of Angela's own heart seemed loud enough to wake the dead—no, not the dead—just an expression! As they approached, she was aware of every creak her saddle made and of Roy's hooves splashing as he crossed the little brook. If anyone were listening from inside, that person would surely have heard her. Sudden fear screamed in Angela's thoughts that she should ride for home—now!

But curiosity seemed to take over her body and all her usual caution, as if she had wandered into one of those really scary movies where someone is standing outside a door and everyone watching is thinking, *Don't open that door!* Angela felt herself innocently, irresistibly drawn to have a look inside. I wouldn't have to actually open a door, she thought, just look inside as I pass. So she looked.

The room was glowing as if lit by a dozen candles, but she didn't see any candles. A figure dressed all in gray, or maybe wrapped in a gray blanket, sat on the floor facing her. He waved. The gray blanket fell behind him, and she could see that it was just a boy, probably a year or two older than she, sitting cross-legged on the floor with bare feet. He had the most serene expression on his face.

13

Maybe he had been doing yoga or something. He had the most beautiful face and perfect hair she had ever seen, his hair kind of silvery platinum in color. Her first thought was that he seemed a little too handsome to be real. He looked very relaxed and at home there. Maybe this was his home. She somehow felt obligated to respond to his greeting or to apologize for her intrusion.

"Uh, hello," Angela answered. "Sorry if I disturbed you . . ."

The boy stood up and walked, or maybe he glided, toward the door. At that movement, Roy Rogers reared on his hind legs, took the bit in his teeth, and bolted for home. As he leaped up the embankment, Angela instinctively grabbed his mane and laced her fingers into it like a burr as she shifted her balance forward with his movement to avoid being thrown from his back. He wove in and out of trees, barely missing their trunks and getting scratched by grasping branches. Amazingly, he didn't stumble once in his headlong charge. It was all a blur and then it was over.

They suddenly burst out of the woods onto her street, and her horse slowed to a normal canter. Angela absolutely could not stop the mustang. He finally stopped, gasping for breath, at the barn gate and turned to sniff her leg apologetically.

"Yeah, I'm still here," she panted. "What was that about? What's with you?"

She slid to the ground and led him to the corral on rubbery legs. She'd have to let him catch his breath and

cool down before feeding and watering him. He paced
back and forth in front of the barn door for a few minutes while she got her own wind back. She led him in a
slow circle for a while, and then as soon as he seemed to
have recovered from the run, she let him into his stall.
And as soon as she recovered from . . . What? What had
she just seen?

4

Home

NGELA GAVE her horse a thorough examination to make sure he hadn't injured himself during his panicked race through the woods. She felt each leg, running her hand carefully down from joint to joint, checking for knotted tendons or cuts. Roy knew the drill and automatically lifted each hoof as she reached it and checked for cracks or stones stuck in the grooves and "frog" on the bottom of his hoof. Next she brushed him with a stiff grooming brush, giving him a bit more time to completely cool down before feeding him any hay or water. Outside, the sky turned completely dark as she worked. The lights at her house, just a short distance from the barn, had been glowing a cheery welcome were being turned off one by one. She really didn't want to stay at the barn alone any longer than necessary after what she'd just experienced, though she was probably headed for a lecture from her mom for being out so late. She now felt sure it had been a bad choice to stay at Marti's so long and not accept a car ride home. Dad would say she was lucky her horse hadn't been hurt.

Her little brother's white pony, Sammy, kept poking his nose over his stall door, snorting for attention and shaking his shaggy mane. "Okay, mister, here's a treat," she grinned as she broke a piece of carrot for him. Sammy wasn't a bit hungry, but he appreciated the attention from his former caregiver. It had been difficult to admit she'd out-grown him, but when Sara Grace teased that Angela could drag her feet to stop him, she gave in and handed the pony down to Brendan. Sammy was a really great little guy and a rare breed in America. He was small, even for an Icelandic horse, so he always had to be ridden in pony classes when shows made the distinction. His pedigree name was Saemundur the Wise after a favorite character from the Icelandic sagas her father often read to his children. Sammy was ancient now, but could still carry Bren on short jaunts through the pasture.

"All right, gents; it's lights out. Time for me to get *my* supper now, if you don't mind."

Angela gave them each a pat on the nose and closed up the barn. As she left she heard them whicker throaty goodnight responses, then return to shaking down wisps of hay from the overhead racks, crunching happily.

Ahead the golden warmth of light from the back door to her house poured out on the cobblestone path

17

that wound through silvery shrubs in the herb garden. The huge old farmhouse with its double-decker porch waited to welcome her home. She left her beat-up boots in the mudroom and hung her coat in the hallway, which led to an immense country kitchen. On one side was a cozy breakfast room next to a stone fireplace where her family ate most of their meals. They took care to have a private space away from the bed and breakfast guests her mom served in the formal dining room.

Angela's mom, Claire, and her two sisters, Chloe and Candace, ran the B & B together. They'd named it The Three Sisters, though they'd thought about calling it The Little Red Hens, the nickname their parents had given them because all three sisters had red hair. In the end, they decided to just put three red hens on their welcome sign instead.

"You never know," her mom said with a wink, "we might become 'the three gray hens' any day now, and we don't want to have to change our name."

Angela opened the double doors of the big shining fridge to find a plate of leftovers waiting for her late dinner. The rest of the family had already eaten and scattered. After warming it in the microwave, she decided to take it to the TV room down in the basement. She could faintly hear people talking and movie music playing. She wanted to tell someone about what she'd seen and about Marti's problems. She hoped her mom was still up. If she scolded Angela for being late, that was fair. She deserved it. But Mom would also listen, and Angela knew she'd end up feeling better. She clumped down the stairs ready

18

to enjoy some company, an overstuffed couch, and a warm blanket on her tired legs. But as she rounded the corner into the room, she almost dropped her dinner on the floor.

Half a dozen drooling monsters with bloody clothing and disgusting facial deformities turned to look her way. The smallest one leaned toward Angela and, with surprising agility for a creature with an axe imbedded in its skull, tried to take the plate from her hands.

"Back off, Bren," she warned as she juggled her dinner away.

"Mumph, hah hah," the nasty thing laughed as it grabbed a couple of morsels in its wart-covered fingers.

The other monsters began to mumble "Me, too" and "I'm hungry." One of them got up and put a bag of popcorn in the microwave on the coffee table and turned it on. A green-haired goblin with a vest made of rotting animal skins opened the mini-fridge and brought out an armload of sodas that it handed around to the group. They all fumbled to open the drinks, spraying little jets of soft drink on themselves in the process. Angela wondered if all little brothers and their friends were this disgusting.

All she could manage was a puny "Ugh, you people are sick" before turning around and heading back upstairs.

"Bye, Sis," the axe-head monster mumbled before going back to the TV screen. The other monsters grunted and turned back to the movie as well. The soundtrack from *Lord of the Rings* followed her up the stairs, and she heard one of her brother's friends snigger, "I think your sister just wet her pants."

5

Ghoulfriends

NGELA MUMBLED some choice words about Bren's "ghoulfriends" before sliding onto the bench in the breakfast nook. Little boys were just weird beyond understanding—especially her brother and his friends. Whatever they were watching or reading, they were sure to latch on to the worst element and decide to make it their fetish. They'd gone out for Halloween dressed as *Orcs* this year, and the costumes just weren't going away, even after most of their candy had been eaten. She really wouldn't have taken much notice of it, but this obsession was becoming a repeat annoyance. They kept showing up in the woods or at the barn unexpectedly in full *Uruk-hai* battle gear and startling her. She was pretty sure they were doing it on purpose, but they swore it was just an innocent coincidence that she hadn't heard them coming.

As she was finishing her drink and feeling sorry for herself about eating alone, the squeak of someone coming up the stairs put her on alert. Okay. If those little geeks wanted to play, she'd make them pay. She grabbed a big blue kitchen apron hanging from a hook by the stove and silently slid into a nook between the fireplace and the door to the basement. *Creak-squeak-creak.* Whoever was coming was almost at the top of the staircase. The door began to open, and Angela sprang forward, throwing the apron over the head of the sneaky suspect crossing the threshold into the room.

"Murmmph, uhhh." The figure under the apron struggled and threw it off as Angela flicked on the brightest lights in the room. "Ha! Gotcha first, you little ghoul . . ." Angela gloated loudly. Then she stopped mid-guffaw. A small woman with carrot red hair appeared from beneath the apron, looking frightened and confused.

"Angela, what in the world . . ." her Aunt Candace began to say, steadying herself against the wall.

Angela wanted to run and hide, she was so embarrassed, but she helped the tiny woman into a chair, apologizing sincerely. Though Aunt Candace was the oldest of the three sisters, she was the smallest; but she made up for her size with energy and pure spunk. She reminded Angela of a leprechaun with freckles.

"Oh, Aunt Candace, I'm so sorry. I thought you were Bren or one of his creepy friends. Are you okay? Did I hurt you?"

21

"Well, well, now I'm fine, dear," Aunt Candace managed to say. "You really got me, though. You would have scared the pants off Brendan, if it had been him, I'm sure."

She started to giggle a little, and Angela felt relief. She picked up the apron and looked at it . . . for some reason it seemed funny now that she knew her mom's elder sister was unharmed by the incident. Candace's short red hair was strewn across her head all to one side, as if she'd been riding sideways in a convertible, and her bright blue eyes still looked a bit startled. She'd actually lost a shoe in the melee. As Angela picked it up and handed it to her, they both burst out laughing.

"Ah, I wish someone had been here with a camera," Aunt Candace said with a sigh. She always said that when any interesting event took place without being photographed.

"Well, I don't think either one of us will forget it— even if we don't have a picture," Angela smirked. "Maybe that would be a good series for you to do sometime. You are the official photographer around here. You could get Bren and the ghoulfriends to help you get photos of people being startled and put them all in one art show or even write a new book about it." Candace had published several books of photography, created as she traveled to different countries with her husband.

"Hmmm, I don't think I would want to be responsible for the reactions I might get when people found out they had been set up for a fright," Candace replied. "Not everyone is as good a sport as I am," she winked. "Nor do they have my robust health—you could stop a weaker person's heart with a shock like that!"

Aunt Candace must be over the scare to joke around, Angela laughed to herself. "I was just about to dig around the fridge for some dessert—can I get you some? What were you working on down there? Aren't you all done with the Mangol wedding?" She sorted through the fridge as she spoke and pulled out a pie plate.

"Oh, yes, I'm done now. I was just working late downstairs in my studio. And I'll join you for something sweet. That was the real reason I came upstairs—not to have an impromptu stress test on my heart. Is that peach pie you found there? That'll do."

They sat back down in the kitchen nook, and Angela served pie and milk. As they ate, the flagstone floor—heated from underneath by hot water pipes—radiated warmth that soothed their feet and legs. As they chatted, the topic turned back to photos of surprised people and Angela said, "Well, if you wanted a look of shock caught on film, you should have been following me on the ride home today. I bet I looked terrified."

"What happened?" Her aunt's forehead crinkled with concern. Angela knew that look.

Her daring trail experiences made fodder for many a conversation between the sisters. She always had to assure them she followed safe riding rules, but if Aunt Candace asked about that tonight Angela would have to confess she'd broken a few.

23

"Well, I think it was just an optical illusion—the sunset can make funny shadows, and you think you're seeing something strange when it's just an ordinary object," Angela said. This is what she'd been telling herself since she got home.

"Ah, yes," Aunt Candace nodded. "Artists use lighting that way intentionally to make some strange pictures—they call it *tromphe d'oeil*, which means "tricking the eye." Any ordinary thing or person can take on almost supernatural qualities in the right light."

"That's probably what it was," Angela said, starting to feel relieved. It was just what she needed: a neat scientific explanation for what she'd seen in the dusk. The giant winged creature had certainly been an illusion. The guy at the cabin was probably just a wandering local kid. She and Roy had been scared by a *tromphe d'oeil*. Just putting a name to something made it less frightening. She looked at Aunt Candace with appreciation. Even though Candace was ten whole years older than her own mom, Angela sometimes felt as comfortable with her as with any of her friends her own age.

"Thanks for being so nice, Aunt Candace. I love you so much. It's been a long day, and I'm ready for a hot shower before this big meal puts me to sleep right here on the bench." She gave her aunt a hug and headed for her room.

Candace watched her go, then paused a moment. That look of concern crossed her face again, and she placed her hand over her heart.

6

The Chalice Moon

CLOUDS OF STEAM followed Angela from the tiled bathroom after she finished her shower. She dove under the poofy down comforter on her bed and scrunched it around her head until only her nose was sticking out. Every muscle in her body melted into the bed. She reached over to click off her lamp, and then took one last look out the window. She thought everyone would be asleep before her, but she could see the silhouette of her mom sitting on the second story porch in a rocker, staring intently at the moon.

An unusual lunar phase must be occurring because the crescent shape isn't vertical, but horizontal. It looks like a cup or a bowl, Angela thought. Mom wasn't rocking, just staring at it. Her long, curly hair fell back over her shoulders, almost looking black instead of red in the moonlight. She had wrapped a quilt around herself and her posture was relaxed, not frightened or curious. Angela decided that her mother was probably just admiring the strangely beautiful moon.

She remembered the scare she'd had and Marti's problem. She really wanted to talk to Mom and considered getting up and going out there. But it was so warm where she was. She tapped on the window, and her mom turned to look. They smiled at each other. She often thought her mom looked like her very own guardian angel, watching over their home in the night. That was her last thought, like a feather falling to the ground, as her eyes closed and she slid farther down her pillow, just barely aware that Mom had come inside and was smiling at her from the doorway.

If she had any dreams that night, she had forgotten them by morning, because the next thing she knew the sun was warming her face as birds chirped frivolously in the trees outside. One thing she loved about the upstairs bedrooms was the quiet in the morning. Spared all the sounds of people walking around and doors opening and closing below, anyone using the rooms could sleep in.

Her horses would be sleeping late, too, since she fed them late last night, so she could stay right where she was. It was lovely to linger longer under the covers on a Sunday. *Linger . . . longer . . . lounge . . . late . . . lovely . . .* Ugh. Realizing she was falling back asleep, Angela shook off the warm comforter and sat up. She rubbed her eyes and blinked in the bright sunshine that formed a square of light over her pillow. A cardinal perched on the arm of the empty rocking chair on the porch outside. It flicked its tail and busily flew off.

She dropped her feet into the white terrycloth slippers on the floor by her bed, scuffed through the bathroom, splashed water on her face, grabbed a warm flannel shirt to wear over her pajamas, and wandered down the stairs into the kitchen. Her mom and aunts were sipping coffee at the breakfast table. A pile of muffins balanced on a plate next to the coffee pot. Angela poured a cup of coffee, plucked a muffin—*ah, still warm*—and carried it to the table. She plopped down on the bench and put her head on her mom's shoulder.

"Hey, sleepy," Mom smiled and gave her a little hug. Mom's auburn hair was looped in a careless ponytail, and she wore a cozy sweatshirt over jeans. Mom wasn't tall and strong, like Chloe, or short and wiry, like Candace. She was right in the middle of her two sisters, like she was in age. "We don't have any guests this weekend, so we're doing our Bible lesson together today. We're just about finished, but you can join us for the exciting conclusion."

Aha. Angela had stumbled right into that one. Now she'd have to hear the moral of the story . . . well, at least she didn't have to sit through the whole thing. Mom, Candace, and Chloe's Bible study discussions were okay for people their age, but too "greeting card-ish" for Angela's taste, like a spiritual lacy apron or one of those ruffled quilted Bible covers carried by the ladies who came to the B & B retreats. The three sisters' talks were like that.

Did that little smirk on Mom's face mean that she knew how Angela felt about it? Mom was so cute when she knew something and she didn't want to let on that she knew. Her hazel eyes would flicker just a tad and she'd look away quickly, as if to keep from laughing, but the dimples in her round cheeks gave her away. Well, if she knew, that didn't stop her at all. She picked up her notes and her Bible, and then she went right back into the discussion where the sisters had left off. "So last night, I saw it again for the first time in ages."

"Really?" Candace leaned in and lowered her voice. "I was watching it from my patio swing. And guess what? I got a photo!"

She pulled a picture from the back of her Bible and laid it on the table. Her sisters leaned in to see, then gasped. Angela sat up to get a glimpse of it. The photo was of the unusual moon her mom had stared at from the porch. So that explained why Candace stayed in her studio late last night.

"The Chalice Moon," her Aunt Chloe said in an almost reverent tone, tracing the moon in the photo with one long finger. Her hands were so graceful and young-looking compared with both her older sisters' hands as they each held a corner of the picture.

"I saw it, too," Angela said as she took her turn holding Candace's photo in her own stubby fingers with their chipped nails. "It was pretty. Um, how is this a Bible study, may I ask?"

"Oh, it's more than just a beautiful sight," said Mom. "The Chalice Moon has a legend. It symbolizes the cup of Christ, and so it stands for our most important eternal truth."

"It's created by light reflected off the Earth," Candace explained, warming to one of her favorite subjects as a photographer. "*Earthshine*, as Leonardo da Vinci called it. The sun's reflection causes the brightest part of the moon to glow, but when sunlight also reflects off the earth and onto the moon, it causes the dark parts of the moon to light up as well, just not as brightly. Then, under the right atmospheric conditions, the earthshine light looks red. When this happens during a crescent moon, it looks like a cup or chalice, filled with red liquid."

"And how this is a Bible study is because 'signs in the heavens' are predicted in many Bible verses," Aunt Chloe added, sitting up so she rose a head taller than her sisters with her upswept strawberry blond hair accenting her height. "You remember a star announced the birth of Jesus. We are supposed to watch for signs of God in all creation, but whenever it has to do with light, there seems to be a special significance, an eternal truth. A signpost that points out something important about to happen."

7

Cowboy Church

ONCE AGAIN Angela felt like she'd come into the middle of a discussion where Mom and her sisters spoke in code about things they all understood. They had so many years together that there were a lot of things they didn't have to explain or repeat. But it left her standing on the dock while they sailed on into waters she'd never explored.

It wasn't like she never went to church or heard the Bible verses they taught. She went all the time when she was a little girl, and she believed her pastor and Sunday school teachers, but she always got the funny feeling they had the same secret codebook her mom and aunts had that explained everything more deeply than they ever got around to telling her. It just seemed like it all meant so much more to them. They talked about Jesus as if he were someone who lived next door, while she felt he was like someone she believed in the same way she did in Abraham Lincoln. He was a good person and the world was a better place because Jesus lived, but he was just a picture in a history book to her. She thought of the way they talked about God as "church talk." It was just the way people talked at Bible studies, she had decided.

"Stick around, Angela, and I'll have an omelet ready to go with the muffins," Aunt Chloe said, cheerily waving a wire whisk as she walked over to the stove where a basket of eggs waited. "Don't worry about the horses; I threw some hay to Roy and Sammy when I fed the chickens this morning."

From the doorway a deep masculine voice laughed. "You don't have to worry about Roy and Sammy going hungry. The only danger those horses are in is from being overfed. Bren and I gave them more hay when we let them out in the pasture just now. No wonder they were almost waddling." Dad rounded the corner from the mudroom in stocking feet and crossed the kitchen to the coffee pot. He poured a steaming cup of coffee, then sat in the big cushioned rocking chair next to the women. His hazel eyes twinkled in his rough-hewn face, and he looked for all the world like a jolly Santa from a Christmas card with his red flannel shirt and apple-red cheeks.

"It must be cold out there," fussed Mom, putting her hand against his cheek and giving him a kiss on his close-cropped blond hair. "Your cheeks are like ice."

"It's crisp—perfect fall weather—just the way I like it." He smiled and rubbed his hands together, blowing on them a little to warm them, then put them on Mom's cheeks and laughed as she shrieked from the icy touch.

"Bren and I went to Cowboy Church, and they just opened the barn doors and let the sun warm the arena."

"C'mon, Dad, it's not called that," Bren called from the mudroom. "It's just The Barn, okay?"

Cowboy Church was pretty much the opposite of Mom's "lacy Bible cover" meetings. It met at Sara Grace's barn around sunrise every Sunday morning, and a lot of its participants were from the horsy crowd in Emerald Circle Valley. It began because Sunday horse shows sometimes kept them away from the usual church services. Since many of them boarded at Sara's barn or met there before vanning to shows together, they got into the tradition of having a short prayer service before they left. Sara's husband, James, was a retired pastor and handy to officiate. He didn't like long sermons, same as everyone else, so they all appreciated his leadership and ability to get right to the point of the gospel.

"Well, I like to think of it as Cowboy Church," Dad chuckled. "Especially when the Country Men are leading the singing."

"Ugh, the Country Men are so corny. That can't be your reason. I think you just like not having to shower and change clothes after a long night," Angela said. "You're not fooling us."

As a farrier, her dad often got called to emergencies on Saturday nights. Equine vets called him when the problem required a blacksmith's assistance, and racing stables called when a horse had thrown a shoe, but had to be ready to run or travel in the morning.

"Yes, having a farrier for a husband is like being married to a doctor without the side benefits," teased Mom.

"What? You don't call this a side benefit?" Dad flexed his huge, really huge, arms for everyone to see and leaned closer to Mom as he pulled up one sleeve.

Mom blushed, of course. Redheads blush about everything, but he really did have a knack for getting her to do it in front of people. Then she'd get flustered and blush even redder because everyone laughed. It was his favorite game. He accused her of having *glowing freckles*.

"That's enough, Noel," Aunt Chloe said, coming to her sister's rescue. "Eggs are ready."

33

8

Eggs and Muffins

A ND THAT WAS enough to end the talking for a while as they all filled plates with food and mugs with coffee or milk. Somehow Bren was first in line, even though he had been farthest from the table. Without his Orc gear, Angela's brother looked very different. His platinum blond hair, big blue eyes, and pale complexion with a generous sprinkling of freckles made him an equal mix of his Icelandic, Polish, and Celtic heritage. Angela suspected that his fascination with gruesome costumes came from a desire to look tougher than his natural baby-faced appearance. He definitely hated it when Mom's friends praised him as such a "beautiful boy." So no one in the family talked about him like that, unless they were trying to bother him.

"Ohho, I'm lucky I got here in time," Chloe's husband, Mike, chuckled as he came down the hallway from their suite on the far side of the kitchen. His dark hair and beard were neatly trimmed and, though his clothes were casual, he was the most dressed-up person in the room. He gave his wife a hug, and she looked up at him adoringly. They were the tallest people in the family, everyone else was just average or below, so it made them stand out in the crowd. The big kitchen's cupboards and countertops were designed with their height in mind, and they were the only ones who could reach the top shelves without a step stool.

Angela believed them when they said that cooking together was their secret to a happy marriage because she'd never seen them happier than when they were creating something in the kitchen together. Uncle Mike didn't cook for a living, but he wrote reviews on restaurants and cookbooks. He said he cooked to relax and to be with his wife. Sometimes he just strummed his guitar in the corner while she cooked, providing "creative ambiance" as he explained. Chloe said it kept her cakes from falling—probably because it kept their two little girls quiet, listening to their papa's music and sitting quietly at the table coloring instead of helping Chloe cook.

Aunt Chloe's six-year-old daughter, Cara, followed her dad into the kitchen leading Heather, her baby sister, by one hand and carrying her doll in the other. She came over to the table in a pink flannel nightgown and bare feet. Chloe scooped her up and Cara's long caramel hair streamed down as she tipped her head back and smiled in her mommy's arms.

"Look, I've caught a mouse," Chloe laughed. "A little hungry mouse that wants a muffin and some milk . . ." She set Cara down next to Angela and scooped Heather up the same way. Heather had wispy platinum curls and hazel eyes in contrast to her sister's brown hair and eyes. After putting her next to Candace, Chloe got them each a muffin loaded with creamy butter.

So the kitchen was now filled with everyone who was at home—with all the happy noise and movement a big family makes when it's hungry and there is a lot of food spread out to enjoy. The only family member not at home this weekend was Candace's husband, Thomas Chester, who was on tour with the Cleveland Symphony Orchestra.

"I'm stuffed," Dad finally said and everyone agreed. They had eaten until they all had napping on their minds.

"That was great, Aunt Chloe," Bren said and clattered some plates into the dishwasher. Everyone did a bit to clean up and then began to scatter to their various living quarters or activities. Angela and her parents and brother lived in the quiet rooms on the backside of the second floor of the house. Chloe and her family had their suite on the first floor off the kitchen with an entrance that opened into the herb garden and a playground area for their girls. Candace and Thomas had converted a summer kitchen off the basement TV room into their suite of rooms, along with remodeling the old coal cellar into a darkroom for her and a soundproof practice room for his drums. It had a private patio with a porch swing that they loved to use on starry nights or when they wanted a peaceful breakfast together.

As Angela turned to go back up to her room to dress, her mom called her aside quietly. "Angela, can we talk?" she asked. "It's not a big deal. But I got a call from Marti's mom yesterday, and I think I should tell you about it."

9

The Talk

MARTI. With all the morning activity swirling around her, Angela had forgotten her friend. "I should call Marti this morning," she said to her mom as they walked up the stairs. She automatically counted the steps of the "back stairs" as they walked—there were twenty-three total, and she had the habit of counting them as she went. Each one had been worn down in the middle by a hundred years of use. They were beautiful, though, varnished golden-brown along with the knotty pine panels on the surrounding walls. She always felt like she was walking up the middle of a giant tree—like Peter Pan's tree house steps. Her mom said they were really the "servants' entrance" to the old house, but that the solid wood paneling would command a king's ransom to construct today.

Each family had their own entrance and exit from the house, to add privacy when it was desired. They intentionally let each other know when they wanted to visit, rather than just popping into a suite unannounced. The big kitchen was the common area for everyone at any time, along with the TV room, the solarium, and the gardens.

When they got to the top of the stairs, Angela's mom turned left to go to her own room, saying, "I'll give you a couple of minutes. Just tap on the wall when you're done dressing."

Angela nodded and turned right to her room. After she'd pulled on a warm sweater and jeans, then washed up, she tapped on the bathroom wall to signal Claire. While she was waiting, she booted up her computer and checked her e-mail. There was a message from Marti, sent early this morning: "Check out my space!" Angela clicked the link and her jaw dropped open as she read Marti's Web page. Mom entered the room just in time to hear her gasp.

"What is it?"

"Oh, this is awful. Look at what Marti posted on her space. I've got to call her."

Claire looked over her daughter's shoulder and sighed. Instead of the cute photo of herself that used to head up her profile, Marti had posted a photo of a garbage can with a discarded rag doll hanging over the side. Next to the picture she had typed: "My new life." She had entered a new blog with the title "I hate my parents!"

"Poor Marti," Mom said.

"Maybe I'd better read this first," Angela whispered.

"I understand," Mom said. "Come get me when you're done."

It wasn't a long blog, but Angela was glad her mom hadn't read it. Marti was angry, and she used some language Mom had never heard her use. Actually, Angela hadn't heard her say things like that much, unless she got thrown from her horse or stepped on. Marti was obviously in more intense pain now, because the words were much more intense. Well, who could blame her? As she said in the blog, her parents were not considering her feelings one bit. They didn't care that her life was being trashed, as long as they got what they wanted. Angela got up and went to Mom's room.

"Don't ever get divorced, okay?" she said hugging her mom and burying her head in her shoulder.

"Don't worry. That's not in the game plan at all," Mom smiled. "Teachers and counselors always tell us that 'kids are resilient' when they want to let us off the hook, but your dad and I think parents are the ones who are supposed to be resilient. We're the adults. We're the ones who are supposed to work problems out. The buck stops here."

She lifted her daughter's face gently and smiled right into her eyes. "We'll think of something to help Marti. Why don't you invite her over for the day? And let her know she'd be welcome to stay with us any time at all."

"Maybe she should just come and live with us until she's done with school," Angela said hopefully. "Bobcat could share Sammy's stall, and Marti could ride the bus home with me!"

"Uh, as much fun as that sounds for you, I'm not sure it's the best thing for Marti," Mom said. "You girls have almost three years of high school left and that's a long time for Marti not to live with either of her parents. Even though Marti's mom and dad might seem like they have abandoned her, they actually need her more than they ever have. She's the one good thing they still have in common. It could bring them back together or at least prevent them from falling apart completely."

"At what cost to my friend, though, Mom? It's not fair for her to have to turn into a psychologist for a couple of people who don't remember they are adults."

"Oh, no. Is that what's going on? She wrote that in her blog?"

"That and a lot of other stuff. Her mom and dad are so selfish! All they want to do is blame each other for their problems and try to get Marti to take sides. She's being torn in two pieces. She doesn't want to have to choose between her mom and dad, but they make her feel that she has to take the side of whichever one of them is talking to her."

"They've stopped talking to each other, according to Marti's mom," Claire said, remembering the phone call. "So they're probably continuing to fight with each other using Marti as the go-between. That certainly isn't fair."

"What else did Marti's mom say?" Angela asked.

"Well, her call wasn't so much about Marti. She was actually worried about you," Mom replied.

41

Phone Calls

M E?" ANGELA was amazed. Mrs. Philips was really confused. Poor Marti!

"Well, she could see this change would be a shock for you, too. Marti's been one of your best friends since grade school. And she really seemed to care about how hard it would be on you. She just called to let me know that if there was anything she could do to make sure you and her daughter could still get together, she'd do everything possible. I think she was just looking for some ideas about how to make that happen."

Angela remained amazed. She was so ready to paint her friend's mom as a villain in all this, and here Mrs. Philips was actually trying to look out for them. "And did you come up with some ideas?" she asked hopefully, her anger toward Mrs. Philips slowly draining away. Maybe the person she thought was the problem would become the solution.

"Well, I just told you my first idea. We'll go out of our way to invite Marti over and talk with her. My second idea has been confirmed by you and by Marti's blog. Mrs. Philips needs someone besides Marti to talk to about her marital problems. I'm no expert with divorce, but I've seen enough to know there are ways to work things out that spare the children a lot of grief. They don't seem to be doing any of those things right now."

"Oh, they aren't." Angela confirmed. "They may not be talking to each other, but Marti says they've been fighting in front of her all the time, and sometimes they throw things or call each other names. She's been spending as much time as possible in her room or at the barn. She's lost weight from not wanting to eat with them, and you know how small she is to begin with. She needs to eat more, not less, but she says even when they aren't fighting, the atmosphere in the dining room is so tense that she's too nervous to eat or gets sick afterwards."

Now her mom looked really worried. "Sounds like her parents are so involved with the pain in their own relationship that they've forgotten how it might affect Marti. And knowing Marti, she's probably trying to act like nothing's wrong, thinking that will help the situation. But that's the last thing they need her to do right now. They need a wake-up call . . . How about if I ask Mrs. Philips to drive Marti over here and you two make

43

yourselves scarce for a while? I'll talk to her mom alone when she gets here."

"That would be great!" Angela held out the phone with Marti's home number already selected.

"Okay, then." Mom smiled and took a breath before pressing the button. "Hi, Lorena? This is Claire . . . you were? What's wrong? . . . Don't you think she's just out riding? . . . Did you call Grace Barn? . . . Sure, I'll go out in my car with Angela. Call us if you locate her."

Mom hung up the phone and looked at Angela, who had already guessed what had happened. "Marti's gone. She's taken a few clothes and gone off on Bobcat. Her mom was just going to call us to see if she was here."

"She might be on her way here," Angela said.

"Let's drive down the road to see if we can meet her," Mom suggested. They both ran down the stairs and out through the garage door, grabbing shoes, coats, and keys as they went. As they drove down the lane, Mom called Dad on her cell to let him know where they were going and why. If they didn't find Marti right away, they'd have to get everyone out on the road in cars to search. It was too cold for anyone in her state of mind to be out wandering—maybe getting lost or hurt.

They drove Mom's Land Rover all the way to the end of the street where the girls usually came out of the woods. They waited a few minutes, watching for Marti and Bobcat to break through into the sunshine. A sinking feeling came over Angela as a thought occurred to her. *What if Marti took the secret path? What if she went to*

44

the cottage to be alone? A rush of memory came back to her from the night before. What if she hadn't been seeing things and there was something to really be afraid of at the old cottage?

"Mom, I've got to get Roy and ride back into the woods. There's another place Marti might have gone to get away, and we can't drive there."

Now Claire had a sinking feeling. What was that look on her daughter's face? Something was very wrong. As they drove back to the barn, Angela quickly filled her mom in on what had happened.

"What have we said about sticking to well-traveled roads when you're out alone?" Mom scolded.

"I know, and I'm really sorry," Angela apologized. "That was all I could think about when Roy was flying through the woods."

45

"And if you'd been thrown off and not made it back? We would have been out looking for you in the wrong places," her mom said. Angela could see she was already picturing the whole tragic scene in her mind.

"But I'm okay," she said trying to delete Mom's picture of her daughter shivering on the cold ground in the dark with broken limbs and wolves howling. *Cut, cut, cut!* Her mom looked like she was about to cry. "Nothing happened, Mom. Don't think about it now. We've got to find Marti."

11

Into the Woods

R OY ROGERS was napping in a sunny spot in the
pasture when Angela came to get him. If it had
been summer, he'd have been lying on his side
stretched out on the warm grass, snoring; but in autumn
the earth became too chilled to make an inviting bed, so
he stood with his head drooping as he dozed. His long,
straw-colored eyelashes flicked slightly as he dreamed—
who knows what horses dream? Probably that they are
eating measures of oats or big crunchy carrots. Roy was
one of those horses that people described as having a personality like a dog—loyal, friendly, and playful. Since they
got Roy from Nevada through the Bureau of Land
Management mustang adoption program, Angela decided
he ought to have a cowboy name. Horses don't get the
chance to watch TV much, so he didn't know anything

about his namesake, Roy Rogers the singing cowboy, or about his "wonder horse" Trigger who was also a palomino. Angela didn't know that much about them, either, but the real Roy Rogers had been a childhood hero of her mom's and Angela liked the name.

Roy's eyelids snapped open when he heard Angela whistle. His head came up, and he started walking toward her before he was completely awake. She didn't have to "catch" him when he was loose in the pasture because he was happy to come when she called—which was really helpful in an emergency.

"C'mon, Roy. We need to hurry," Angela said as she slipped his everyday blue nylon bridle over his head. Luckily for her, Roy hadn't rolled in the mud yet, so she didn't need to brush him. She checked his hooves for stones or muck, but they were clean. Great. She placed both hands on his back and vaulted up without bothering to get a saddle. Angela was just as comfortable without a saddle since she'd learned to ride bareback. They took off down the road at as brisk a pace as she dared without warming up her horse first. She just hoped they'd find Marti in time. She really hoped that her friend wasn't in the cottage and that no one else was, either.

Mom insisted that Angela take her cell phone with her, although they both knew reception in the area was unlikely. There wasn't anything more she could do, knowing that the route was inaccessible by car. Roy was the only horse they had that was trailworthy. This was exactly the reason she and Angela had agreed to the rule of riding only

47

on paths that were near passable roads when going out alone. If something happened on a remote trail, they could end up with the exact problem they were now facing. Claire watched as the girl and horse disappeared down the road and felt more helpless than she ever had in her life.

Angela turned Roy onto the steep path that led to the cottage. He resisted at first because they never took that path on the way to Marti's house, only on the way home. He was a creature of habit and balked at changes in routine. Angela felt his hesitation was ominous because she was used to trusting his instincts on the trail. If he didn't want to go a certain way, it was probably because there was trouble ahead. He had a natural instinct for roads that had been overwhelmed by spring floods or downed trees long before she could see them. And he reacted if there was a herd of deer or a coyote ahead before she could have spotted them. His skills probably saved his life when he was growing up in the mustang herd out in the desert. The Bureau of Land Management had rounded him up and sent him to Angela to civilize. She respected his intuition and had learned to read his alerts. The mustang didn't balk at rabbits or water or anything safe, like horses did that had been raised in barns and trained in corrals. He saved it for real trouble. And he was balking now.

"C'mon, Roy," Angela coaxed as he tried to back off the trail. "Marti and Bobcat need us." She clucked her tongue and turned him from one side to another, squeezing her heels and calves into his sides until he gave in and walked into the woods. His ears flicked back and forth like radar dishes, and every muscle in his body was tense, but he trusted his rider as much as she trusted him. He plunged down the bluff and through the woods. Suddenly, he caught a scent in the wind and planted his feet for a moment, lifting his head and snorting. He neighed loudly. From the clearing ahead an answering call sounded—Bobcat!

Now Roy charged ahead. Soon Angela could see the black pony cantering toward them, neighing in greeting with an urgency that suggested a call for help. But where was his rider? His reins were streaming behind with no one holding them and the saddle was empty. Its stirrups banged against his sides, like an invisible rider spurring the pony on. His neck was glistening with sweat as if he had been running at top speed and his eyes were wide with fright.

As they met on the trail, the two horses whickered and put their noses together in greeting. Bobcat stepped up to Roy's side and put his forehead against the big horse's neck as if for comfort. It gave Angela the opportunity to catch Bobcat's reins without needing to get down from Roy's back. She walked them both a few steps down the trail to see if the pony was limping or hurt in some other way. Outside of being winded, her friend's mount seemed to be okay. She decided to take that as a good omen.

49

12

An Unexpected Meeting

ALL RIGHT, Bobcat. Let's go find Marti," Angela said and turned him back in the direction he had come. At first the pony resisted, making it clear he'd hoped to keep going away from whatever had scared him. With a little "horse whispering" from her and peer pressure from Roy, she convinced Bobcat to let her lead him down the trail. When they got to the point where she could see the cottage roof, Angela remembered Roy's last reaction to the stranger at the cottage and decided to tie each horse to flexible tree branches and continue on foot. She and Marti had taught both horses to "ground tie" so they'd usually stay where she dropped the reins without wandering, but she didn't want to take any chances this time. She left them out of visual range of the cottage, hoping they wouldn't see anything to frighten them.

As she came near the clearing, Angela began to run. Marti was lying on the porch of the cottage and a figure in gray was bending over her. A shock of silvery hair hid his face from view, but he looked like the guy she'd seen the night before. What was he doing with her friend? Was he covering her with his blanket? What was wrong?

"Hey!" Angela yelled. "Marti! Marti . . ."

Thank God! Marti turned her head toward Angela. The stranger looked up and smiled at her. It was the same guy she'd seen. But before he smiled, she was sure she saw him flash a look of anger. What was he hiding behind those perfect teeth?

"We've been looking for you . . . Are you okay?" Angela asked her friend as soon as she reached the porch. She didn't see any blood or anything. But something was wrong. Marti stared at her as if she'd never seen her before. Then she blinked several times and her normal expression returned.

"Angela," she said faintly. She stared in Angela's direction as if trying to focus on her.

"I'm afraid Mar-tee took a bad fall," the boy said softly. He pronounced her name as if it was a foreign word for him. His other words were perfectly unaccented. "She will be fine now." He withdrew a thin gray blanket he had covered Marti with to show she was unharmed.

"I'll be fine, Angela," Marti answered as if echoing the boy's words.

"You are Angel?" the stranger asked, looking at Angela as if he didn't believe it. His eyes were dark, almost

51

black, and he had long platinum blond eyelashes that matched his hair. His complexion was pearl, almost gray, as if he never went out in the sun.

"I'm Angela. She's probably just stunned. Did you get the wind knocked out of you?" Angela asked her friend.

Marti was starting to look normal. "I guess so . . . Clay helped me . . . after I fell . . ."

"Oh, thanks," Angela said to him. "I've seen you here before."

"Yes, I watched you riding across the hill, and I saw you come to this place. I'm afraid your horses don't like me, for some reason," Clay smiled. "Yours didn't like me any better than Mar-tee's did. He took you to your home very fast, didn't he?"

"Uh, yeah, he did. Well, speaking of home, we should be going home now," Angela said hastily. "Our parents are out looking for us. Are you okay to walk, Marti?"

"I think so," Marti said, sitting up.

Angela took her hand to help her stand up. It was as cold as ice. Marti managed to stand but swayed just a bit before getting her balance. Clay stood back, stepping into the shadow of the doorway. He wasn't much taller than Angela, which put him at about five foot five. "I'd help you to your horses," he said, "but I don't think they want to see me again."

"It's probably better if you stay here," Angela agreed. "Do you live around here?" She wanted to ask him what he was doing at the cottage, but anyone had as much right to be there as she did—maybe more.

"Yes, I'm from around here," he answered mysteriously. Fine. If he wanted her to mind her own business, that was okay with her as long as he left her friend and her horse alone.

"Goodbye, Clay," said Marti, looking over her shoulder as they walked away. The stranger just watched them go from the shadowed house without answering, and then disappeared inside as they left his view.

"Is that guy living there?" Angela asked.

"Maybe," Marti answered. "He said something about it belonging to his family or his people or something like that. He said he's been watching people who come into the valley. I don't know. I was sitting on the porch trying to talk to him and find out what he was doing there when Bobcat freaked out and ran off."

"Wait, you were on the ground already when Bobcat took off? I thought he threw you," Angela said.

"No, I was sitting on the porch at the cottage talking to Clay . . . Bobcat took off when Clay came out of the house."

"He was inside?"

"Yes," Marti remembered. "He was just sitting on the floor at the back of the room. I was sitting on the porch thinking and didn't notice him for a while. When I did, I said "Hello," and he just talked to me from there. Bobcat probably didn't see him until he came outside. Clay must have startled him. That was when he took off."

"So how did you fall?"

"Huh? I don't know . . . but I was falling, I remember. Everything went dark, then I saw Clay's face. It

53

looked like it was at the end of a tunnel or something."
Marti looked confused again. Then she shivered and, for
some reason, it sent a cold chill down Angela's spine.

She studied her friend's pale face and then had an
idea. "Have you had anything to eat today?"

"Well, not really," Marti admitted.

"Here!" Angela pulled a granola bar from her coat
pocket and gave it to her friend. "You probably fainted
from hunger, dummy. At least take some snacks when you
decide to run away from home!"

"There wasn't anything edible left in our kitchen
outside of ketchup and mustard." Marti peeled away the
wrapper and devoured the whole bar. "We've been order-
ing take out a lot lately," she mumbled between bites.

They arrived at the place where Angela had left the
horses and got a warm greeting from them. Now that she
saw them, Angela wondered how Clay knew they were
there. Could he see them from the cottage? She looked
back, but could no longer see anything but the roof.
Maybe he heard them when they whinnied to each other.

"Let me help you up." Angela started to help Marti
into the saddle; there was no sense in taking the chance
she'd faint again. As she boosted her friend up, she noticed
an unusual necklace that slid out over her collar when she
bent to mount the horse. "What's that?"

"Clay gave it to me. He said it would protect me,"
she said, pulling the silver chain all the way out into the
sunlight. A crystal charm dangled on the end of it. "Isn't
it beautiful?"

13

Found!

ANGELA STARTED to protest about accepting jewelry from a boy she'd just met when both horses started to act up. They struggled to get away as if they were going to run back to the barn without their riders. The girls grasped the reins firmly and were glad their feet were still on the ground. Then they heard a sound they both knew was trouble, and it was already too close to avoid. One of the worst hazards of riding trails was motorbikes—four-by-fours, minibikes, or trail bikes. Their riders usually weren't watching for horses and certainly couldn't hear them coming, so the horse people had to watch out for bikes flying at top speed over crests of hills or around blind turns on remote trails. The one they heard coming was almost upon them. They moved the horses off to the side of the path and Marti put her hands over Bobcat's ears.

Angela got as much eye contact as she could with Roy and commanded, "Stand, Roy." He did the best he could to obey, standing in one place but trembling from head to hoof.

A green Honda trail bike zoomed into view from the valley below. The rider stopped the bike just before reaching the girls and turned it off. This did little to calm their mounts, but it was better than going by them full-throttle, like some of the bikers did. The rider pulled off his helmet, revealing wavy black hair and a tanned, square-jawed face. He flashed a smile of superiority and said triumphantly, "Finally found you!" It was Billy Joe Countryman. Ugh.

He planted his gaudy cowboy boots on the ground and pulled a walkie-talkie out of his leather jacket. "Homebase, this is Lone Ranger. I've got my eyes on the prize. Repeat. I've found the girls."

"Roger that . . ." was all they could understand of the static reply. But it was easy to tell his brother Chuck was on the other end.

"Understood! Meet at Highland Drive crossing. Out," Billy Joe said back. Then he turned to Angela and Marti with attitude and started giving orders like he was an arresting officer. "Okay, girls, everyone will be waiting for us at the trailhead. We'd better get going."

"Hey, that's just where we were going before you spooked our horses with that piece of junk, Billy Joe," Marti scolded.

"Yeah, we were doing just fine before you came along," Angela agreed. Billy Joe was so smug. He was a couple of years older than they were, so he felt obligated to remind them of every possible rule when he was working at Grace Barn. He was actually a good-looking guy, but he was so annoying because he knew it. Sara Grace probably sent him out to look for Marti after her mom called.

Before he could say anything else to provoke them, another voice called from the other side of the path. Out of the shadows, Angela's dad and Bren jogged over to them. Angela had never been so glad to see them, but she felt a twinge of guilt that they'd come so far only to have to hike home again. If only the cell phones worked here, she could have saved them a trip.

Dad wasn't the least bit put out, however. He hugged both of them and said, "We're all just thanking the Lord that you're okay, Marti. Your parents are waiting with Claire back at the road. They were worried sick about you, honey."

Even Bren wasn't complaining about the long run. He always enjoyed being his dad's sidekick on any adventure, but he usually took any chance to gripe about something Angela was doing. Not this time. Instead, he volunteered to help. When Billy Joe offered Marti a ride home on the back of his bike, Bren said he'd ride Bobcat back for her.

She didn't want to do it. She thanked Bren for the offer, but said she'd have no trouble riding. She didn't thank Billy Joe, who looked disappointed.

"Tell you what, Billy Joe," said Dad, "it's a long walk. I'll take you up on that ride back. Angela, you could put Bren behind you on Roy."

57

"I can walk," Bren protested. "I haven't explored this trail before. I'd like to have a look around."

Angela glanced over her shoulder toward the cottage. She had a bad feeling about leaving her little brother anywhere near it. What had that guy Clay meant about watching people who come and go in the valley? Creepy. Was he watching them now?

"C'mon, Bren," she coaxed. "I'll even let you sit in front and hold the reins. You'll be the one giving me a ride."

Bren was onboard when he heard that. His big sister never let him ride Roy. He threw up his arm for her to grab, and she let him use her foot for a stirrup. He tried not to look too thrilled as he took up the reins. Even though he tended to pester her, Angela was one of his heroes. Not that he'd ever admit it aloud, even under torture.

Dad and Billy Joe pushed the bike a few yards before starting the engine. The horses weren't surprised by it now that they'd seen it. They were happy to head toward the barn, so they didn't need to be urged on, just held to a moderate pace. They were soon at the road. Billy Joe was gone when they arrived, but Dad and Mom were there with Marti's parents. Angela was thinking how awkward it would be for them to scold her in front of everyone, but Mr. and Mrs. Philips didn't give any lectures. They just hugged Marti and actually apologized for "how everything's been so difficult lately."

Angela looked at Mom. She'd had plenty of time to talk to them during the wait, and it looked like she hadn't wasted her breath.

14

The Secret Room

WHY DON'T we keep Bobcat at our barn tonight and let Marti go home with her parents in the car?" Claire suggested. Marti agreed and gratefully collapsed into the leather seat of their Lexus. Mrs. Phillips put her arm around her exhausted daughter. Bren switched to Bobcat's saddle, glowing with satisfaction that he got to ride both coveted horses in one day. As Angela turned to follow him back to the barn on Roy, she smiled over her shoulder at her mom. Claire smiled back as she pulled away in the car and gave her daughter a nod. A good end to a difficult situation.

Back at the barn, Roy announced their arrival with a loud whinny, and Sammy returned the call from a corner of the pasture where he was grazing. The shaggy white pony ambled slowly. He nodded his head in excitement as he saw Bobcat, who snickered a hello. Sammy wasn't the jealous type, after a succession of young equestrians had been his riders over the years. He was just as happy to see Bren riding Bobcat as to see Bren alone. Either way, he was likely to get fed.

Bren, however, was feeling a little guilty. Here he was riding a flashy, young Arabian while his good, old buddy was lounging in the pasture with burrs in his mane. "Hey there Sammy, old boy," he said, rubbing the pony's forelock and giving him a piece of fuzzy, melted candy from his pocket.

"Candy is no better for Sammy's teeth than it is for yours," Angela teased, putting on her best imitation of Mom. She swung down from Roy and fussed over the pony, too.

"Oh, Sammy, you know better. Tell Bren to get you some sweet feed instead of candy. Just say no, Sammy."

"Ha! Fat chance of that pudgy pony passing up a treat," said a voice behind them. They turned to see Billy Joe strutting down the path from the house.

"What are you still doing here?" Angela said, irritated to be surprised by him twice in one day.

"Well, if you must know, I was invited to stay for lunch as a reward for all my hard work searching for you and Marti," he answered, smug as usual.

It figured. The Countryman brothers loved to eat, so Sara Grace was more than happy to get them invited to eat somewhere other than her house. She always had a table full of people with her own family and the foster

60

children she sponsored—troubled kids who came for equine therapy after school or boarded at the facility through Children's Services. Grace Barn's slogan was "The outside of a horse is the best thing for the inside of a kid." The Countryman brothers had been a part of that program as kids. They had survived a car accident in which they had been seriously injured and their parents were killed. The Graces helped them heal, both physically and spiritually. Billy Joe and Chuck graduated to mentoring younger kids when they became teens. They considered the Graces to be their second family and Grace Barn their home. They both had natural talents in music that the Graces encouraged by letting them play for Cowboy Church and other events. Although Angela didn't like that style, she had to admit the brothers were good "if you like that kind of music."

"So, your mom sent me to get you guys for lunch," Billy Joe continued. "Ready?"

"Go ahead, Angela," Bren said. "I'll untack Bobcat and let him loose in the pasture with Sammy and Roy. We can come back and feed them after dinner when they've had a chance to cool down."

"There's no rush. I'll help you," Angela said, throwing Billy Joe a sharp look. "If you're too hungry to wait, just go on to the house." Bren was pretty good at taking care of his horse alone, but Bobcat could be a handful.

"Sounds like you're trying to get rid of me! And after all my work to find you today, I thought I'd get a hero's reception from you, Angela Clarkson. What's a guy gotta do to get some respect around here?"

Many scathing replies leaped to Angela's mind, but she decided to keep them to herself. He had a point, she guessed. He had just been trying to help, even if it did serve his purpose to have some fun flying around the trails and wasting gas on his noisy bike. She didn't want to be unreasonable and get too aggravated with him. It had been a scary day, and her emotions were on edge. That guy at the cottage and Marti's story about him gave her the creeps.

"Sorry. And thanks for your hard work. By the way, did you notice anyone at that old cottage on the path just before you found us?"

Billy Joe threw her a curious look immediately and leaned forward. "No, did you see someone there? What happened?"

"It was just a guy. He had been talking to Marti before I came. I'd seen him there once before and wondered if you had ever met him. His name's Clay."

"Don't know anyone by that name—you've gotta be careful talking to strangers out on a deserted trail, Angela. You've got no cell reception and no walkie-talkies. Two girls all by themselves. That's not good. What did he want? What was he doing there?"

Oh, brother. Angela was afraid her peace offering of a thank you was about to backfire. Just a tiny spark was all it took for Billy Joe to start bossing people around. "Listen, it was nothing—just a guy out walking or something. He was trying to be helpful."

But Billy Joe was already off and running with a new adventure in his sights. "Well, give me a description, and I'll look into it for you," he declared. "Holy cow! You and Marti really need some looking after—"

Angela cut him off. "And you're just the man to do it, huh? Billy Joe, if you want to get anywhere with Marti, you need to back off on the hero stuff. She's a capable horsewoman, not some girlie princess from the mall." Angela picked up Bobcat's saddle and bridle after Bren finished unbuckling them, turned her back on Billy Joe, and headed for the barn.

Billy Joe looked at Bren. "Huh?"

Bren shrugged. He could see Billy Joe was clueless about women, but he wasn't going to hear that from a ten-year-old like himself. They caught up to Angela and pulled the heavy barn door open for her.

The barn was small and at least as old as their farmhouse. The heavy wood door had been set on modern hardware with a rolling track, but it was made when carpentry was serious and things were built to last. Like all the wood in the barn, it was weathered to a soft finish inside. Under the wooden frame of the barn was an even older stone foundation and floor. Angela lugged her burden to where they kept the tack in a small room at the back of the stable. Bren called it "the secret room" because the door leading to it looked like part of the wall.

Billy Joe looked surprised when Angela opened it, like everyone who saw it for the first time. "That's a neat trick. I'd never have known there was an extra room back there if you hadn't opened it."

Here was something about which Bren *could* tell him. "We found a book at the library that said this farm

63

was part of the Underground Railroad. We think the people who owned it must have hidden runaway slaves in the secret room. There are even some drawings on the stones by the floor that look like a map for them to follow. It shows what stars to look for and places to hide on the way." He pointed to the drawings that were etched on a cornerstone at the back of the room. Bren had researched the history of the movement to help slaves travel to free lands and hide from bounty hunters. He thought it was one of the more exciting things about the old farmhouse, so he had checked out several books on the subject for his summer reading list.

Billy Joe bent over the drawings that looked like they were made from a shiny silver ink in the shade of the little room. In the first one, a group of stick figures were walking toward a larger one who pointed to a star formation in the sky. "Cool! These are really interesting. Y'know, they look a little like some ancient Native American paintings I saw at the Serpent Mounds near Columbus. Those stars are the Big Dipper, aren't they?"

"Yes," Bren said. "The slaves called it 'The Drinking Gourd.'"

Billy Joe smiled and sat back on his boot heels. He started singing in a deep, slow voice, "Follow the Drinkin' Gourd. Follow the Drinkin' Gourd. Well, the old man is waiting gonna carry you to freedom. Follow the Drinkin' Gourd . . ."

It gave Angela chills. Weird. Billy Joe didn't sing in that voice at Cowboy Church. She couldn't help thinking his voice was nice . . . that she was listening to a talented guy who could sing any way he wanted. She wondered why he'd limit himself to one kind of music, since country and western style was all she heard him sing at The Barn.

"Wow, that's great, Billy Joe," Bren said. "You really can sing—even without your guitar or anything."

"Okay, you can get his autograph later," Angela said, breaking the spell. She tossed Bren several flakes of hay for the stalls and scooped some sweet feed from a covered bin. "Let's go get some dinner before it's cold."

15

Epiphany

HEN THEY got to the kitchen, Billy Joe's brother, Chuck, was already sitting at the table along with the rest of the family. Chuck was two years younger than Billy Joe, but barely any shorter. Both brothers were over six feet tall, and Chuck had a more husky build than Billy Joe. He also seemed to be working on growing a mustache that was faintly visible at this point. His brown hair was gathered into a ponytail that he usually covered with a cowboy hat or baseball cap when he was not at a dinner table. It flew out like a flag when he rode in barrel-racing competitions.

Chuck had trained his buckskin quarter horse, Pumpkin, to work without a saddle and bridle. The pair could compete just as easily without any tack against any contestant using full gear. They started training together that way when Chuck was just ten. Sara Grace helped train Pumpkin to go tackless to make riding easier for him because Chuck had lost his left hand and forearm in the car accident that killed his parents. As he grew bigger it would not have been a problem for him to put a saddle and bridle on Pumpkin, but Chuck found that riding without tack was a great way to show off and "psych out" his competitors. Since his low-withered horse was as cushy as an old sofa, there was no reason to add the extra weight of a saddle. He always said, "If I can get Pumpkin to do anything with just leg cues, why bother with all that other stuff?"

Chuck called out to Billy Joe, "I've saved you a seat right next to the pie." He pointed to a huge chicken potpie that was steaming and ready to cut, another of Chloe's masterpieces. Angela sighed with relief when she saw only one empty seat next to the one Chuck had saved, and Bren followed Billy Joe to claim it. She'd had enough of Billy Joe and didn't want to have to answer any new questions from Chuck.

She wished she could think of a way to sneak off with some dinner and not have to sit in on a big family discussion about the excitement of the day. Everything had turned out all right, and she was tired. She especially wished she could get her mom away from the group and talk to her alone. What had Mom said to turn the situation around with Mrs. Philips? Was everything fixed? Was Marti's life going to go back to the way it was?

Maybe Mom and Dad had told everyone to take it easy with the questions, because the conversation at the table never got around to the afternoon's adventure with Marti. Everyone praised the food, especially Chloe's wonderful piecrust, and talked about mundane things. As soon as they finished eating, Angela's mom caught her daughter's eye and headed for the room they called "the library." It was a sunroom that ran across the west side of the house, a place full of books and overstuffed chairs next to a view that overlooked a Koi pond and the Emerald Circle River Valley below. When her mom held writers' retreats at the B & B, they used the room for lectures, prayer meetings, Bible studies, and discussion groups. When they weren't using it for guests, her mom would often do her own writing and research there, rummaging through the stacks of books and making notes on stickies and in spiral notebooks instead of on her computer.

"Sometimes I like to look things up in real books, made of paper and binding, instead of electron streams," she explained. Angela knew Mom would probably write in pencil instead of on a computer keyboard if she could get away with it. Writing was something spiritual to her, a way to think and pray. She always remembered a lecture her mom gave to groups of writers in that room. Holding up a glass bowl of differently shaped beads, she'd say:

"There are moments, little morsels of time, that make up all our years on this planet. Like a bowl full of natural pearls, they are experiences of different shapes and colors. A writer chooses which of those moments to use to tell her story as if she were stringing them into a necklace. It's not that the ones she chooses are necessarily more important than other moments she left in the bowl. So she looks at how they fit together and creates a particular design from linking them in a certain order. She can start again, trying to create other stories from further arrangements of pearls. It's just a matter of choice. No choice is right or wrong. It's just her choice."

Mom had picked a cozy couch next to that glass bowl to sit on and patted the cushion to invite her daughter to join her. "I'm stuffed," Angela said as she plopped down on the cushion. "And worn out. But I'm not too tired to ask you some questions. What happened? What did you say to Mrs. Philips?"

"I didn't have to say much," Claire answered. "When they thought something might have happened to Marti, both her parents had an epiphany. I just helped them understand some *whys*."

"What's an epiphany? Isn't that a church holiday or something?" Angela asked.

"Yes, there is a holy season of days by the same name. And it celebrates something similar to what we mean when we say someone's had one. It means you understand something profound—it's defined as 'a leap of understanding' in the dictionary, as I recall. In this case, I think Marti's parents suddenly understood what their troubles were doing to their daughter—to their only child. In that moment, they had a choice. They could decide to ignore what they had discovered or to act upon it, to grow from it. I just helped them see that to ignore it would be a great loss."

69

This was starting to sound like deep water to Angela. She wanted a simple answer. "So are they getting back together, or what?"

"Well, that's not a decision they could make in one day. The things that have brought them to the point they are at now have been going on for a long time, so it will take some time to untangle the knots they've made in their relationship. They may have the patience for it, or they may not. We'll have to pray for them and see what they choose. I suggested that the Graces might be able to counsel them. For today, the decision they made was to care for the innocent people around them who may suffer for what they have done and are going to do."

"So they have decided to act like grown-ups?" Angela asked.

"That's a good summary!" Her mom smiled. She hugged her daughter and they sat there for a while, listening to the family wrapping up lunch and watched the afternoon shadows grow longer as the sun headed toward the western rim of the valley.

16

Horse Stories

A LITTLE SOUND like the meowing of a kitten interrupted the conversation, and they turned to see Cara and Heather. Chloe's girls were everyone's babies and they obviously loved it. Angela couldn't resist their round cheeks and dimples. Heather was crawling on her hands and knees, pretending to be a cat. She pounced up on the couch with her sister close behind.

"Miss Melissa and I fed our horses," Cara told Angela, holding her doll up so she could be included in the conversation. "Did you feed yours?"

"Yes, Miss Melissa, I just did that very thing before lunch," Angela said, talking to the doll on cue. Cara looked delighted and nodded Miss Melissa's head.

The girls had a pretend stable of Breyer horses under the nightstand in their bedroom. They played with them

for hours, imitating everything they saw Angela and Bren
do with Sammy and Roy. They even mimicked Dad's
blacksmith routine, bending horseshoes out of aluminum
foil and crimping them around the model horses' feet.
The girls watched everything that went on in the house
and worked it into their pretend world, where they were
the horsewomen, cooks, photographers, or musicians.
They turned the house into the whole community, walking around the pantry like it was the grocery store, com-
menting on the prices of the items they were loading into
their toy shopping cart and using a spatula for a price
scanner. They made the home library into a public library
where they would take turns playing the librarian, offi-
ciously checking out books and declaring the due date
and fines for overdue books.

72

The girl who played the part of the patron taking
out books never minded paying any fines, however,
because she always had a purse full of pink toy money
that she'd happily count out like she owned the bank.
They were royalty in their imaginary world, and no
expense was too great, unlike the real world where Chloe
informed them of her "treat budget" before leaving the
house: "You may choose one treat each." Or, "We're buy-
ing a toy for your friend's birthday today. Remember, this
isn't a shopping trip for toys for you. It isn't your birthday this week."

Budgets were important to the success of the
extended family at The Three Sisters. Everyone worked
hard at their separate professions, but they all agreed that
wise planning and conservative spending were just as

important for the B & B to make it. All the kids picked up on that mindset from the start. They all helped as much as they could, contributing sweat equity to restore the old farmhouse into a masterpiece. It had taken a lot of sweat: cleaning the neglected yard and barn, painting, refinishing old wood, repairing old plumbing and wiring. The family was serious about making the place into the most attractive retreat in the county. They had a lot of riding on the decision after changing their careers and lives so their families could work together in the same town.

Chloe, who was in charge of the cooking, swore the kitchen they'd finally created rivaled any professional kitchen she'd ever cooked in during her years as a chef. It would have cost a fortune without the skills they all had combined to build it. Even Angela had helped by searching Internet auction sites for the equipment Chloe needed and building materials at bargain prices. She found great deals on cabinets, countertops, and appliances from restaurants that were remodeling and builders' closeouts. When she haggled the sellers down to even lower prices than they'd listed them for, her dad just shook his head and laughed, "Angela reminds me more of Amma Brenna all the time!"

Amma is the Icelandic name for *Grandma*, so that's what Angela's dad's mom wanted to be called. Brenna had married Captain Jack Clarkson when he was stationed in Iceland while flying helicopters for the U.S. Air Force. As a young woman, she had been excited about coming to America with her husband, but she was in for quite a shock when her husband's next assignment took them to

73

the hot, dry climate of Nevada. She made the best of it over the years they lived there. She also fulfilled a little childhood fantasy of becoming a cowgirl when she learned horseback riding at a local stable. She had the right personality for a cowgirl; she talked like "a straight shooter"—no frills and to the point—and it became a family legend that Amma Brenna could "horse trade" for any item her family needed and come out with the best deal anyone had ever heard of. Her most famous deals were literally horse trades because she had traveled back to Iceland and purchased several Icelandic horses to begin a breeding farm. That was how Sammy, Saemundir the Wise, came to America.

When Noel, their first son, was ten, Brenna decided he was strong enough to take care of a pony and bought Sammy for him. After being passed down through three boys who outgrew him one-by-one, the pony lived a life of semi-retirement along with Amma Brenna and Grandpa Jack on their farm in Tennessee. Angela, Noel's first child and Amma's first grandchild, started playing with Sammy as soon as she could walk and started riding before she was old enough for kindergarten. On her ninth birthday, she explained to Amma Brenna, at great length, why she felt she was old enough to take care of the pony alone. Her arguments were successful, and Amma agreed to let her take him home. So that was how Sammy left the farm in Tennessee and came to Ohio. He was passed down to Bren when Angela grew too tall for him.

17

Web Spinner

S AMMY AND Roy want you to give them a bath," Cara told Angela. She liked to talk about two of her toy horses that looked like Sammy and Roy as if they were the real things.

"Oh, I should really do that," Angela said, playing along. "Are you and Heather going to have a bath with them?"

"Meow, meow," agreed Heather, still playing kitty.

"Aw, kitty, do you like to take baths?" Angela laughed. Kitty Heather nodded and kept up the mewing. Chloe came in from the kitchen and immediately seized on the opportunity to make bath time part of their game.

"Come kitty-kitty," she called to her little daughter, "let's take a bath with the horses."

The girls were ready to go for some fun, and Cara took Angela's hand to bring her as a horse bath assistant. Angela couldn't resist; they were so cute.

While the girls gathered up their tub toys and Chloe ran the bath water, Angela decided to take a quick look at her e-mail on Chloe's computer. There was a new e-mail from Marti that read, "Check out my page." When she clicked the link, a new web profile photo of Marti appeared. The sad trash can photo had been replaced with a smiling web cam shot. Marti must have just taken it today, because it showed her wearing the crystal necklace Clay had given her. Next to it, she had changed the title to "My new life!" and entered a new blog with the title "Thanks to my friends!"

"A-a-angela-a-a!" Cara called from the echoey bathtub.

"I'm coming, just a minute." Angela clicked the blog title. She guessed she was about to read a thank you from Marti to all the people who had done the searching today, but she was surprised to read:

Today I found that friends are the most important thing in this world—even new friends. I met someone today who opened up a whole new world to me. I felt like I had lost everything until I met him. He gave me the crystal necklace you can see in my profile pic. He said if I believed, it would keep me safe. The minute I decided to trust my crystal, help came to me. I felt like I was alone and lost in the world, but when I believed, friends and family came to me as if they had been called by the crystal. I received the answer to my cry for help, to my heart's desire, to my prayers. Now I believe in a greater power than myself. I have a new peace that I've never had before. May peace come to you, too, as you read this.

"Whoa!" Angela sat back and dropped her hands at her sides. "What in the world . . ."

"Hey, the girls are ready for their favorite cousin to play," said Aunt Chloe from the doorway. She stopped when she saw the look on Angela's face. "What's up, Angela?"

"This is completely weird. Here, read what Marti wrote in her blog."

Chloe looked over Angela's shoulder. "Wow! That does sound strange. Who gave her that crystal?"

"Well, I don't really know this person. He's someone we met on the trail. I thought he was just trying to help Marti when she fainted, but now it sounds like he talked her into some cult or something . . . Do you think it's possible crystals really answer prayers?"

A hearty splash came from the bathroom followed by giggles. Chloe turned to look. "Uh, come in the bathroom, and we can talk while I keep an eye on the girls. I don't want them to start a flood in there."

They went into the bathroom. The two little girls had lined up their toy horses along the bathtub and were plunging then into the bubble bath one after another. "Look, Angela, it's just like a pond, but with bubbles," Cara giggled.

"Bu-u-ubles, bu-u-u-bbles," Heather chanted and laughed as she dipped a horse in.

"Yeah, those horses will really smell nice after a bubble bath," Angela encouraged them and then turned to Chloe. "So what do you think about crystals? Lots of kids wear them at school, but I thought they were just a decoration."

"Not necessarily," Chloe said, shaking her head slowly. "There are people who wear them for good luck or consider them some kind of transmitter for spiritual energy. Different groups use crystals in their religions. If you're asking me if I believe in them, then my answer is no. Prayer is answered through Jesus alone. It's not by using a good luck charm or chant or even by going to a certain place."

"Well, whether you do those kinds of things or not, how do you know if God's answered your prayer or if things would have turned out all right anyway?"

Chloe smiled and patted Angela's shoulder. "That's where faith comes in. The Bible says we need to believe in Jesus first, and then we'll know he answers our prayers. That's important because it takes faith to understand he's answered us when his answer doesn't come the way we expect it to."

"Mommy, Mommy, will you get us more horses?" Cara pleaded.

"No, honey," Chloe answered.

"Please, please, please?"

"No, that's enough stuff in the tub. There's hardly room for you two in there with all the horses you have now."

Heather joined in the pleading, "More, more, more!"

"Hey! That's enough." Chloe pointed at the girls and gave them her "serious" look. "Don't beg after I've said no and told you why."

Then she turned back to Angela. "There you go. It's just like that. If we don't really know what the Bible says about Jesus and we don't trust him, we'll keep on praying for our own way—even when he's said no for our own good."

"So you think that's why people want crystals? Because they want to control the way things turn out instead of accepting an answer to prayer that's different from what they asked for?" Angela asked.

"I do. I think you hit the nail on the head. Real prayer is risky. You let God know your desires and then you have to trust him for the outcome. My girls trust me because they know me. Even if I don't say yes to every whim that passes through their heads, they have learned that I can be trusted to take care of them and do what's best for them."

The little girls looked up at Angela. They were covered with bubbles, so cute and so happy. Who wouldn't want to do the very best thing for them? Hmmm . . . if she could feel so much love for her cousins, even though she wasn't perfect or anywhere near it, wouldn't a perfect God love them, and herself, ten times more? "Is that why the Bible says we should be like little children? Because they trust us?"

"I think so," Chloe smiled. "Jesus taught people to understand God by using things they could see in everyday life. He made it simple enough for a child to understand."

Heather must have picked up on their conversation because she started singing "Jesus Loves Me" in her sweet baby voice. Then she raised her little hands and waved them as if she were directing a choir. They all joined in to delight her, and Angela had the thought that it was the best church service she'd been to lately.

18

Brother Bren

KNOCK-KNOCK, knock-knock, knock-knock . . . it sounded like a woodpecker had perched on the outside of Angela's bedroom door. "What? What?" she mumbled, looking around to see if it was really morning already.

"It's me," Bren said through the door.

"Okay. Come in . . . What do you want? What time is it?" She was so sleepy she couldn't remember where to look for her clock.

"It's already six," he answered. "C'mon, we've got to feed the horses."

"Ugh, we don't have to go so early . . . Give me thirty more minutes," Angela said, disappearing under her down comforter.

Bren was not to be denied. "No, c'mon. We have an extra horse to take care of!"

So that was it. Bren was excited about Bobcat being there. Angela knew she should go with him. Even though he was good to take care of their two horses on his own, Bobcat was a registered Arabian, and he acted like it. He was more "flighty" than their calm "grade" horses. He was likely to shy at little noises that Roy and Sammy would ignore. Roy had been a little like that when they first got him because of the wild environment he grew up in, but his basic temperament was calm. The warm-blooded breeds, like Arabians, needed experienced hands to reassure them.

"Dad said I had to get you if I wanted to go to the barn," Bren coaxed. "So, c'mon. Let's go."

"I hate Mondays," Angela griped as she felt around on the floor with her toes to locate her slippers.

Once Bren saw her up, he bounced out of the room. "I'll be in the kitchen. Hurry up and I'll put a piece of toast in for you."

Angela grabbed some jeans and a sweater. It looked cold outside and not quite light yet. She could still see that funny moon the aunts and Mom had talked about. It still looked like the bowl of a goblet of wine. She scuffed into the kitchen and could smell toasting bread. Bren had two glasses of orange juice poured. He must really be excited to do all that for her. When the toast popped up, he actually spread the butter and strawberry jam on her piece, too.

Though Angela's stomach wasn't really awake enough to feel hungry yet, she decided it would be good to encourage her brother's generosity. "Thanks, Bren. This is great. So you're pretty excited to see Bobcat again, huh?"

Realizing he was busted, Bren blushed, "He's a cool horse. I loved riding him yesterday. Not that Sammy isn't just as good! He's my best pal, ol' Sammy. It's just that Bobcat is bigger and faster."

Poor Bren was clearly torn between loyalty to Sammy, who was like a friend he'd known all his life, and this exciting new stranger. But Angela could see that Bobcat was the wrong horse for Bren right now. Even if their family could afford a purebred, which they couldn't, the Arabian needed an experienced rider with a very light touch. Bren wanted to ride like a rough and tough cowboy, but at the same time he needed a mount that was patient and forgiving. Angela looked at Bren and suddenly realized that Roy would be the perfect horse for Bren to grow into someday. If and when she went away to college, it would be perfect if Bren would take over as Roy's rider.

83

She put her hand on his shoulder. "You know, Bobcat is a great pony, and he's close to horse-size, but I think your days on ponies are numbered. By the time I was twelve, I could see that I'd look too big on a pony. I'm not tiny like Marti. She'll probably be the right size for a large pony even when she's grown up. You are already taller than I was at ten. You're on the way to being taller than I am now."

"Really? Are you sure?" Bren sounded amazed.

"Yeah, I can see it by how tall you sit on Sammy. And his children's size saddle that I had plenty of room in at your age is already starting to look small on you. We ought to think about moving you up to the next size this spring so you can get used to it before the summer shows."

Bren's face lit up like it was Christmas or something. Angela could see how much it meant to her brother that someone thought he'd grown. It was probably hard for him to see any progress, standing among his friends who were all bigger than he was. They were all growing steadily together, so maybe none of them realized how much. In a couple of years they'd probably pass her up—man, she hoped they'd outgrow the scary costume phase before that. Meeting little Orcs in a dark hallway was bad enough—She didn't want to run into any that loomed larger than her!

Bren put on a regular coat and boots today, leaving his goblin armor behind. *Good. Progress*, she thought. He grabbed a couple of carrots from the fridge and followed her outside. As they tramped down the path, the faint sun battled to rise above the gray clouds on the horizon. Its pale yellow glow didn't look capable of warming anything soon, and they could still see their breath in the cold air.

"Look, I'm smoking," Bren giggled, holding up a carrot and blowing out puffs of warm air.

"You better not smoke, or you'll stunt your growth!" Angela laughed.

"Not if I just smoke carrots!" he said. Yeah, so she didn't have to worry about him growing up *today*.

As they walked down the path toward the barn, Angela remembered how Bren had worked with her to fix it up. When her parents, aunts, and uncles were remodeling the farmhouse together, they put Angela and Bren in charge of cleaning out the little two-stall barn, so they could move their two horses from their old place. The barn's roof, walls, stone flooring, and doors were solid and in good repair, so knocking down cobwebs and chasing out a few mice was the main job. The barn was cozy and had a sunny window in each stall. The pasture fence needed repair in a few spots, so Dad helped hammer in new boards and reinforce some posts. Angela and Bren searched the area in and around the two-acre pasture for poisonous plants and trees. After they cut down several choke cherry trees and carefully dug out some poison ivy, they let the horses out to run and graze. The first thing Roy Rogers did was lie down in the soft grass and take a nap. Sammy grazed as much as he wanted, and then lay down for a nap next to his friend. Everyone could see that the new tenants had officially approved the barn!

The horses heard them coming and neighed a greeting. After opening the big barn door, Angela could see that the three were quite cozy inside. They radiated so much heat that the air in the little barn felt far warmer than the pasture air. Sammy and Bobcat were especially cozy, their two warm bodies heating the air in one stall. They poked their noses, one black and one white, over the door, expecting a treat from Bren. Barn cats, looking like little muffs or furry pillows, lay curled on each horse's back, toward the rear where the perch was most cushy. Their game was to creep along the rails of the stalls until they were level with a resting horse's back and carefully slip onto it. Angela guessed the horses must like it, too, or they'd never have allowed it. It was always a funny sight on chilly mornings, as well as a sure sign that winter was almost here. She might have to get out a stall blanket for Bobcat if he stayed another night. His sleek coat never got as thick as Sammy and Roy's. They'd grow fluffy enough coats to look like furry bears before the winter was over.

The cats loved Bren, and they pounced over to him. They twirled around his legs, purring and mewing, waiting for him to open the big canister where their food was kept. At the moment, there were five cats: a gray tiger stripe, a brown tiger stripe, a calico, and two black-and-white spotted shorthairs. Bren filled a big bowl with dry kibble, and they stood in a circle around it, dipping their heads like a bunch of kids bobbing for apples.

Angela grabbed hay from the last bale on the floor in the secret room. There were only four flakes remaining, so she'd need a new bale tossed down from the hayloft. Bren stopped feeding carrots to Bobcat and Sammy and climbed the ladder to the loft to get a new bale without being asked. The hay bounced once as it hit the floor, a sign it had been baled nice and tight. When Angela clipped the two loops of twine that held it together, the bale sprang open, giving off a scent that smelled like a warm summer day.

She unclipped Roy's black rubber water bucket and headed for the barn door to throw out the leftover water. She swung the bucket, getting set to launch the murky water over the fence.

"Whoops, hold up there!" her dad cried as he came around the corner at the same moment. He caught the bucket midswing and spared himself a soaking.

19

Lucky Shoes

O H, SORRY, Dad! I didn't hear you coming!"
Angela said.

Her dad wasn't usually so quiet. They'd hear him
whistling or humming or talking to his beagle-pug mix
dogs, Ginger and Peachy, or to no one in particular as he
went about his work. *He must be tired*, she thought. And
the puggles weren't with him. Maybe he was up all night
and just coming back from a call.

"I came to see how Marti's pony is doing this morning," he said. "You said you found Bobcat running from
a scare, so I wanted to make sure he's sound today. Have
you walked him around yet?"

"Not yet, we were just feeding him. But he seemed
fine when I rode him home yesterday," Bren answered.

"You're probably right. Just to be on the safe side, let's have a quick look and make sure he hasn't loosened a shoe or anything. You know the old saying, 'For want of a shoe, a horse was lost. You can't be too careful with a horse's feet and legs."

Dad opened the stall door and led him out, being careful to block Sammy from charging out at the same time. In the open foyer of the barn they had crossties in place for grooming their horses. Bren shut Sammy's door and handed Dad a rope from each side of the aisle to clip onto the metal rings on the sides of Bobcat's halter so he couldn't wander to the right or left. As Dad checked each shoe to make sure it was securely fastened in place, he ran his hands down the pony's legs to see if any of them felt warm or had lumps in the tendons or muscles.

"His shoes look good, but his right foreleg feels hot. See, right here." Dad showed Bren where he'd felt heat and let him touch it and compare the temperature to that of the other front leg. "Let's see how he goes."

They unclipped the ties and led Bobcat around the level ground outside. "He's not actually limping," Dad said as he walked the horse in a straight line. "But watch his head as he walks. Each time that right hoof touches the ground he nods his head a little. If you didn't pay attention to that and rode this horse, you'd see him limping by the end of the ride."

Bobcat was already tossing his head and restlessly moving his hindquarters from side to side. He wanted to be set free to run in the pasture, now that he'd had breakfast. From the way he was acting, a little leg strain wasn't going to slow him down much.

"He wants to run, but we'll need to keep him in this morning. I'll wrap his leg with a cold pack and take it off after my nap," Dad said, leading Bobcat back to the crossties. "You two lead Sammy and Roy out slowly after I wrap his leg. Lead them until they are out of sight from the doorway. If he doesn't see them take off running, he won't be as disappointed when I put him back in the stall."

"You can put him in Roy's stall so he has a little more room to move around, and I'll let Roy stay outside," said Angela. "If Bren brings Sammy back in after a few minutes, he can keep Bobcat company from the other stall." Roy was already developing that shaggy winter undercoat, so he'd be warm enough in the pasture until the afternoon sun began to fade. The great thing about mustangs was their hardiness. They were almost as tough as Icelandic horses.

Bren fed Bobcat wisps of hay and a few carrots while Dad wrapped a chill pack on the leg. Dad distracted him the same way while they led the other horses outside. Sammy and Roy loved to run and buck on a crisp morning, and this morning old Sammy even pranced a bit as Bren led him. As soon as Angela unhooked the lead line from Roy's halter, he cantered away and kicked up his heels a few times. She and Bren ran back to the barn door and quickly slid it shut, so Bobcat wouldn't see the other two horses when they circled back around by the barn.

Angela and Bren watched while Dad adjusted the wrapping on Bobcat's leg. She smiled as she observed the familiar routine. Dad had a natural skill with horses that made them comfortable with him right away, but he had also been trained at The Ohio State University's famous farrier school. He loved throwing around heavy tools and beating metal into shape. When he had free time, he enjoyed creating metal sculptures or reproductions of antique tools or carriages. Because of all that voluntary lifting, all he had to do was flex his arms slightly and his muscles would show right through his shirt, and the veins on his hands and forearms would bulge.

His big arms were part of the story Angela's mom often told about how they met. When he came to the stable where she kept her horse, all the girls who boarded there lined up to get their horses shod and loitered around watching the handsome young farrier at work. "They were all boy-crazy that summer, so your handsome dad and his massive arms were a huge attraction. I have to admit that I was impressed, too, but my friends were so giggly that I was embarrassed to be seen with them. They had a meltdown when he asked for my phone number, even though he said it was to check back with me about a custom shoe he could make to correct a problem in my horse's gait. I was more impressed that he knew about that than I was by his muscles . . . but they were also impressive. I really couldn't help noticing," Mom had admitted, blushing slightly.

"Yeah, I was in the right place at the right time, and I said the right thing to get your attention," Dad had added. "And look at us now." Dad always gloated about his good fortune in finding Claire and getting her to become his wife. He made it clear that he considered his marriage to her one of his life's successes.

"Dad, do you believe in luck?" Angela asked as they put Bobcat in the stall.

"Luck?" He lifted his red OSU baseball cap and scratched his head. "Well, if you mean the kind that gamblers at the track think they have, I'd say no. I do think some things turn out for the best when I least expect them to—that's what I think of as 'lucky.' But I think we make our own luck by making wise decisions or by planning ahead—like checking your horseshoes before riding."

"Well, aren't horseshoes supposed to be lucky?" Bren asked, returning with Sammy on a lead rope. He pulled on the latch to Sammy's stall door that Dad had made from a heavy horseshoe welded to a slide bar.

"Now that particular horseshoe is what I'd call 'making your own luck.' I put that there to lock down the door so smart Sammy won't figure out how to slip the bar out and open it. So we've been 'lucky' in that your pony hasn't gotten loose—and you've been 'lucky' to have such a clever old man to make things like that for you," Dad grinned, scratching his old pony's fuzzy nose over the door.

"So you don't think there are things that give you luck, like four-leaf clovers and crystals and stuff?" Angela said.

"I don't. People who use good luck charms are wishing, but I believe in praying. People who wish usually talk about affecting 'fate' or 'destiny' and believe in a 'higher power' that's some unknown force. People who pray usually feel they are talking to God as a real person who showed us what he is like through Jesus' life. So if you know what Jesus' life was like, you will get a good idea of what God is like. And if you know what God is like, you'll know what kind of prayers you can expect him to answer."

Bren was on board with Dad's explanation. "Pastor James said the same thing once about praying in God's will. He said you have to ask for things that will please God if you want your prayers to be answered. And you have to read the Bible to know what pleases God."

They started walking back toward the house as they talked. Angela liked how simple that philosophy sounded, but she'd seen some complicated prayer situations that weren't so easily explained. "What about people who don't get healed? The Bible says Jesus healed everyone, right?"

"Well, think about that a minute." Dad replied." "When the Bible account says Jesus healed all who came to him, it was on specific days in certain towns. It doesn't say every person in every town he walked through got healed. There's another verse that says he couldn't do great miracles in one town because the folks there didn't believe in him."

"Also, just because we live in America and think the ideal things are to pray for are to be healthy and have money, that doesn't mean that's God's will for everyone at every minute of their lives. We always want everyone's life story to flow smoothly along like a feel-good movie, but sometimes there are deeper issues at work."

Angela hung up her coat and pulled off her boots as she thought about that. "I think Chloe was trying to explain the same thing to me last night. Are you saying that sometimes we just don't know what we ought to pray for because we don't really know what's good for us in the long run?"

"That's right," her dad said. "But I'll tell you what I think is good for me right now . . . a warm breakfast and a nap! I was up half the night at Grace Barn. I need a rest before someone else calls me with an emergency. You two get off to school, and I'll check on Bobcat when I wake up. Tell Marti it doesn't look like a serious injury, but she might want to van him home or leave him here a couple more days."

Bren's face lit up at the news. He beat Angela up the stairs in several bounds. His week was starting out just great!

93

20

The Tenth Grade

THE TARDY BELL for Angela's homeroom rang at seven-forty, so she really had to hurry. She ran through the shower, threw on some clothes, and tucked her damp hair under a wool hat as she raced back down the stairs and out the door. Her uncle Mike was waiting with the car already warmed up to give her a ride on his way to work out at the gym. Bren's school started an hour later, so he would take the school bus with his ghoulfriends.

"Thanks for the ride." Angela said as she shut the door of Mike's sporty silver Pontiac.

"Thanks for keeping me on schedule," Mike smiled. He considered it an "occupational hazard" that being a food writer required sampling food that put on pounds if he didn't exercise every day. He had told Angela she could count on him for a ride to school this year, so he'd be forced to get up and head for the gym for an hour every day.

In no time they pulled up at Emerald Circle High's drop-off drive. "See you tonight," Angela called as she hopped from the car.

She spotted Marti at the door waiting for her, like every day. Her friend looked so happy today, a real change from the past month or two. Angela remembered what her mom had said about the damage to Marti's parents' marriage happening over time, and she realized Marti hadn't been looking this happy since school started. *How long has she been keeping all these problems to herself?* Angela wondered.

"Hey, how's Bobcat?" Marti asked as she shouldered her book bag, and they started into the school.

"My dad checked Bobcat's legs and said he might have a small strain." Angela pulled off the wool cap and shook out her long hair. "But he said it didn't look serious. He iced it this morning and he'll recheck it at lunch."

"Oh, your dad's so great. I really didn't worry about Bobcat for a second last night."

"Good. How did it go with your parents?" Angela asked.

"It was good. They didn't say a lot, but I could tell they were trying to work things out," Marti answered hopefully. "Maybe we won't have to move after all . . . I'm going to believe for that. I'm going to call the family who want to buy Bobcat and ask them to wait a couple of weeks to close the deal. Maybe something will change . . ." She pulled on the crystal hanging from its silver chain as she spoke.

They slid into their seats in the last aisle in homeroom. Ms. Fitly was starting to take attendance, so everyone else was breaking away from little groups by the doorway and finding their places, too.

"What does 'believe for that' mean?" Angela asked.

"My crystal . . . I'll tell you at lunch," Marti whispered from her chair behind Angela's.

Great! Angela could not imagine that conversation. She didn't want to discourage Marti from believing in something spiritual and from feeling so positive about her family. But that crystal might be a problem, according to what she'd heard from Dad and Chloe.

Angela slumped down and opened a workbook. They were supposed to use the first twenty minutes of the day for "time management" and to finish up or check the homework that was due. It took about thirty seconds to check her planner for her daily to-dos, so that left the rest of the time for homework. She looked over her French exercises—a bunch of verb tables to fill in and matching vocabulary words with definitions. The answers she put in Friday looked just as correct today. She looked up a few in the textbook and was glad she did it. Three corrections. Hmmm. By the time she finished, the bell for first hour rang. She turned around to Marti and said, "See you at lunch." They both had to sprint to their first classes because they were at opposite ends of the school.

It was torture to sit through three classes waiting for lunchtime to come. Angela looked out the window during

French, the last class before lunch. Five minutes passed like thirty. Madame Corbeau was droning on and on about conjugating a verb in the past tense, *le passé composé*. Her delicate fingers fluttered across the letters on the whiteboard, and the tiny, gray-haired woman in her tailored lavender suit looked more as if she should be giving a seminar on how to prepare a proper tea than giving a grammar lesson. Angela tried to concentrate. Although she liked the petite teacher and her lovely French accent, her imagination refused to cooperate today. A red bird flew across the window's view and Angela's eye was drawn to it like a magnet.

The wide vista seemed to open up to her as if she were flying with the little bird, as if she'd gone sailing out the window. Wouldn't everyone be surprised if she suddenly flew out the window? She looked around the room and saw the class concentrating on what Madame was explaining. Would they look the same way, have the same expressions on their faces, puzzling over how she had managed to fly out the window? Oh, no. That would be too funny. Angela dropped her face and put her hand over her mouth so Madame Corbeau wouldn't see her smile, but it was too late. One giggle escaped before she could stifle it.

"Mademoiselle Clarkson," the teacher said, her friendly face suddenly marred by frown lines. "You are amused by something?"

"C'est un oiseau," Angela answered in French, hoping that doing so would make things all right.

Madame looked around the room for a bird. "Ici?" she said, thinking the bird was inside.

"Dehors," Angela responded pointing outside.

97

"Regardez ici, Mademoiselle." Their teacher lifted one manicured finger that held a beautiful silver ring with a lavender stone and pointed to the writing she was doing on the board. "S'il vous plaît!"

"Oui, Madame." Angela no longer felt like laughing.

After class, Madame Corbeau handed Angela an extra worksheet "for practice," explaining it seemed like she might have missed out on part of the lesson. Great. At least it was finally lunchtime. And it was Monday, so there would be pizzaburgers—if she hurried. The cooks never made enough for the whole student body, so halfway through the last period—Angela and Marti's lunch slot—kids would have to settle for tuna surprise or whatever else might be served.

"C'mon, c'mon," Marti waved as Angela rounded the corner.

"No running," Mr. Bowan cautioned as they passed him in the doorway into the lunchroom. The tall, gray-haired principal had positioned himself at the entrance to the lunchroom hallway. He was about to retire at the end of this year, so he said everything in a semi-retired way. And everybody paid semi-attention. Marti and Angela joined the stampede to the lunch line.

"There's still a whole tray left," Angela told Marti, standing on tiptoe to look at the lunch choices that remained. She counted the people ahead of them in line. Maybe they'd each get one if a couple of people got salads or cheeseburgers instead. The salads looked good, but always tasted funny, like someone had sprinkled powdered aluminum foil over them. Still, some of the girls were always on diets . . . she looked at the line to see if any super skinny girls were in front of them. Not really.

"I'm starving. That smell is driving me crazy," Marti moaned. She put her hand on her belly. Then she had an idea. She moved her hand to the crystal necklace and closed her eyes. Was she praying or something?

"What are you doing?" Angela hoped nobody had noticed it.

"You'll see," Marti answered mysteriously.

They got to the food counter and picked up two worn plastic trays. Mrs. Owczarek was handing over the last pizzaburgers to the two people in front of them. Ugh. They were about to be stuck with rubbery cheeseburgers or bitter salads. Disappointment was all over their faces. The lunch lady looked at them kindly. She held up one finger to signal them to wait. They watched her ruffled blue hair net disappear around the corner. When she came back, she was holding another half-tray of pizzaburgers that she laid under the warming light in front of them.

"SCORE!" yelled the kid behind them in line.

"Dere you go, girls," Mrs. O said in her thick Eastern European accent. "You vant pitza, yah?"

"Thank you! Thank you!" the girls both said at once.

"Yah, that's good, I vant you to eat all the lunch. No leaving vegetables on plate this time, okay? Here, have some more green peas and carrots. You eat dem all, yah?"

"Yes, Mrs. O," they promised.

"Good girls," she smiled.

They slid their trays to the cashier and Marti looked back at Angela and winked. "See that?"

21

Pizzaburgers
and Inner Peace

ANGELA DIDN'T say a word. They took their trays to their usual table by the window. Simone and Teri moved closer together to give them more space next to Michelle. Adam and Kyle stared at their trays from across the table.

"You got pizzaburgers!" Kyle said, adjusting his glasses to make sure he was seeing clearly.

"How did you manage that?" Simone asked, shaking her dark curls. "You were at the back of the line."

"It's a secret!" Marti said laughing. "But I'll tell you what it is."

Oh, no, Angela cringed. Would they think Marti was crazy? She had everyone's attention now, for good or bad.

"I met someone who gave me this," she said dangling the crystal from the end of its chain. It picked up light from the window and split it into tiny rainbows that reflected across each face in the circle of kids as it turned. "Crystals draw positive energy toward you and break up negative energy. So if you want something to happen, you can attract it to you by thinking about it and directing your thought to the crystal."

"Are you serious?" said Michelle.

"I got a pizzaburger just now, didn't I?" Marti took a big bite. "Mmmm."

"Are you really saying you think we got these pizzaburgers because of your crystal?" Angela asked.

"Of course. You saw me. I concentrated on getting pizzaburgers for us while I was holding the crystal. Suddenly, Mrs. O decided to bring out another tray—a secret tray, I say—I bet she was saving it for the teachers, but she gave it to us. It was the power of my thought."

"Great!" Adam cheered. "Does it work on quizzes? I have one next period in German."

To answer his question, Marti held up a quiz from math that was marked with a 90 percent score at the top. Everyone turned and looked at everyone else. Could it be true? Marti was terrible in math.

"So you aren't going to give any credit for that to all the studying you did last week?" Angela asked. "I remember you also went in for tutoring."

"Hey, I'm not saying you don't have to study or do any work at all . . . but this isn't the only thing. My parents got along all day Sunday, and they haven't done that in months. They both stayed at our house, too. It was the first thing I wished for, and it came true right away."

Angela didn't want to burst Marti's bubble, but it didn't seem fair that she also didn't give any credit to Angela's mom for the talk she had with them. Still, she didn't want to discourage her friend from being hopeful and having faith of some kind.

"And what about you, Angela?" Marti continued. "How did you think to look for me at the cottage when I usually take a completely different path? I thought of you and wished for help—and you came!"

"Sounds like the ol' Jedi mind trick to me," smirked Kyle. "It only works on the weak-minded, you know ..."

102

Angela made a stink face at him. Kyle was one of her favorite friends, even if he was a guy. He was sort of a nerd; he liked Star Wars, and he was a computer and math genius, but he was a lot of fun. His big glasses made his slim face look even thinner, but he was blind without them. He hadn't had the growth spurt most of the other boys his age already went through, so he was still the same height as Angela. It was safer for him to hang around with their group and a nice guy like Adam, who wouldn't take advantage of his size and push him around.

Simone, Teri, Michelle, and Adam were in the marching band together. They all played saxophone, so they were a tight group. Tiny, dark-haired Simone played a black nickel tenor sax that looked huge on her petite figure, but she was a fierce player who could burn up a piece of jazz music better than anyone else. Teri and Michelle both played alto sax. The two girls made a striking contrast when they played together; Teri, tall and blond, and Michelle, almost as tall with silky black hair down to her waist. Adam carried the band's huge baritone sax, but it almost looked like a tenor-size instrument on his tall frame. He was definitely big enough to be on the football team, but he preferred music to sports.

Angela and Marti got to be friends with all of them at band practice at the end of summer when they had brought their horses to several marching practices. Roy and Bobcat had to get used to the band so they could carry the flags for some of the parades. The two horses seemed to like being team mascots. They pranced and arched their necks in true parade horse style. Angela and Marti were sure it wasn't just the extra treats the band members brought for them that got the horses excited, but that was probably a feature they liked as well as the music and marching.

103

Last year a couple of other girls with horses also carried flags, but they had forsaken the group when they "outgrew" their interest in riding and sold their horses. Angela could see them, Kelly and Jill, sitting with "the cool kids" at the other side of the cafeteria. They were working on posters for a dance that was coming up. That's what they thought was fun now that they'd given up riding. It was a big "So what?" to Angela.

"I know what you mean about believing in good things," Teri said. She tossed her long blond hair over her shoulder as she leaned forward and said in almost a whisper, "I really want to think that way, but sometimes I just lie in bed awake and worry about the world ending or dying young or getting sick. Sometimes I just can't stop my mind from running stuff like that over and over until I can't sleep. Doesn't that happen to you guys?"

Everyone mumbled agreement, but they were shocked. Teri had everything going for her: a nice family, a beautiful house, talent, and good looks. Of their whole group, and maybe of the whole school, she should be the one who felt most secure. They all assumed she didn't have a care in the world. Everyone stared at her. If Teri didn't have it all together, what hope did any of them have?

But Marti recovered quickly and pressed her argument. "That's exactly the point! You have to believe in something bigger than youself, even if you're at the top of the charts. You can't just trust in yourself."

"So what are you talking about—God? Space aliens? Nature?" Michelle asked.

"All those things together, I think," Marti answered. "God is just one name for the ultimate power in the universe, whatever you feel comfortable picturing that as being."

Kyle spoke up. "Whoa! Now I just have to step in here and tell you that's not what the Bible says about God. Maybe you all go to church somewhere that doesn't teach from the Bible, or you don't go anywhere, but once you start talking about God, you should include the Bible in your discussion."

"Our church teaches from the Bible," agreed Simone. "But I don't think I've ever heard them say anything against crystals or nature or anything."

"Yeah, there are actually plenty of people in the church I go to that believe crystals or copper bracelets or magnets can heal them," said Michelle.

"I read that we all have fragments of magnetic minerals in our noses that help us have a sense of direction—all animals do," Adam said. "Scientists think it might help animals and birds migrate, so they go in the right direction. Maybe it can do other things naturally like help people heal."

"Well, there are magnetic fragments in all living things on Earth down to tiny worms," Kyle said. "That's why scientists suspected there might have once been life on Mars. They found rocks from Mars that had magnetite arranged in the same patterns they'd seen in invertebrates on this planet and thought they might be fossils of primitive life that had once lived there. But naturally occurring minerals that help organisms function aren't supposed to be worshipped. They are just part of the Creator's design."

"Don't be so closed-minded, Kyle," said Teri. "I think it's great Marti is getting into her spirituality."

Just then the bell for class rang. "See you after school," Angela called to Marti, who didn't act like she'd heard, but they always met out front before going home. Angela walked off to class wondering what she ought to think or say about all that. Well, maybe she would figure something out in the next three hours.

105

Angela never got the chance to talk to Marti again that day. At the beginning of her last class, a student aide brought her a note from the office. It read: "Angela Clarkson, please come to the office to meet your father."

The halls were empty and her footsteps echoed as she walked toward the principal's office. In various classrooms she could hear teachers lecturing or students answering questions. Some turned to look outside when they heard her footsteps, clicking like tap shoes in the quiet hallway. Mr. Bowan was coming the other direction and heading for the same door.

"Well, hullo, Miss Clarkson," he called out in his friendly southern accent. "How are you today?"

"I'm not sure," Angela answered. "My dad came to get me early. Something must be wrong."

"Well, I hope not. Let's just see about that," he said, putting a hand on her shoulder and looking right into her eyes with concern. He opened the door for her and there was Dad, holding his baseball cap in his hands and standing by the reception desk. He looked anxious.

"Angela," he said, giving her a hug. "We have to go to the hospital. It's Aunt Candace. She's having some serious trouble. The rest of the family is already there. I came to pick up you and Bren so you wouldn't come home to an empty house."

"Oh, Dad! What's wrong? She seemed fine yesterday." Angela couldn't believe it. Candace had battled cancer seven years ago, but she seemed to be over it.

"The doctors aren't sure yet. She was giving a photography seminar in the library when she began having some heart pain and trouble breathing, so they sent an ambulance right away. The paramedics thought she might be having a heart attack."

Angela burst out crying. She couldn't help it. *Not again, not again!* she thought. Dad put a big arm around her to lead her out of the office.

"We'll have someone bring your books and assignments over tonight," Mr. Bowan promised as he held the door for them. "Don't worry about a thing. You go on and help your family."

They jumped into Dad's truck at the curb and headed to Bren's school. Angela waited in the front seat while Dad went in to get him. She put her head in her hands and prayed, "Oh, God, please help Aunt Candace. Please help her. We all need her well and with us."

22

Emergency

NGELA, BREN, and their dad were silent on the drive to the hospital, processing the news and their reactions to it. They bumped along the country road squeezed in together on the bench seat of Dad's truck. Bren looked scared, his light complexion faded to pale. Angela put her arm around him. She thought she knew how he was feeling because when Candace had been diagnosed with cancer, she had been about the same age he was now. She remembered how difficult it had been to understand what was going on and how helpless she felt to do anything about it.

It was a short ride to the little community hospital, and they were all anxious to get there and learn what they could do for their aunt—if there was anything they could do. When she had been fighting cancer, the whole family had taken turns keeping her company and helping in practical ways when she was weak or alone. Thomas had cut his symphony tours at first, and then had returned to touring as her health improved and her extended family looked after her. He was the featured percussionist for the Cleveland Symphony Orchestra and, although they had no lack of talented people waiting in line to fill in for him, his unique style was greatly missed by the orchestra and audiences whenever he could not perform. Candace said the percussionist was "the heartbeat of the orchestra" and that Thomas' great heart fueled their masterpieces. When he played, Thomas' passion for music washed over the audience like a tide. His dark complexion and hair were the visual opposite of Candace's, like their personalities—his was one of seriousness and intense concentration with few words, hers was sparkly and flashed from one idea to another like a bird. "We are the perfect combination of chocolate and champagne," Candace explained.

109

Angela was sure he'd be home soon if it turned out that Candace's problem was serious, because Thomas always said he could not play his best unless his "muse" was well. He called her his muse, and she called him the same because they each inspired the other's work. Before she had cancer, Candace had always traveled with him, giving him her support and taking photos of exotic cities and people. But she had needed more rest since the illness, so he had limited his trips to shorter tours since he had to go without her much of the time.

Angela thought the story of how they met was one of the most romantic she had ever heard, although she didn't go in much for romantic stories in general. They had met when he was playing a concert at the Paris Opera House. Thomas had been playing a solo on stage— as he stood alone in the spotlight and created his dynamic music, Candace lost her breath and her heart. She was there on assignment to photograph the orchestra and had been issued a backstage pass to take some candid photos of the concert. She said she "shamelessly exploited" her duties to meet him in person and the rest was romantic history. After being married for fifteen years, they said they still felt as in love as that first night they had met. She had just gotten an e-mail from him saying Paris was "dreary" without her, which had delighted her. "Oh really, Thomas! Imagine anyone thinking Paris is dreary, no matter who is missing," she said. He had replied with an e-mail saying, "Paris can never really be Paris without you." Angela and the sisters all sighed when she read it to them, of course. So romantic!

Candace and Thomas never gave birth to children of their own. At first they were too busy with their careers, then later the cancer made conceiving impossible. They weren't without children in their lives, however, because of the nieces and nephews and because they mentored many young music prodigies and art students interested in photography. Angela had fallen into two categories because she was both a niece and was fascinated with Aunt Candace's art. She followed her to outdoor photo shoots, carrying extra bags and props and learning about filters and film speeds. When they'd do darkroom work, Candace said it reminded her of herself as a child when she used to watch her own mom and dad do photography. They'd had a little studio and had taken photos of the town's babies and families for years as their own three daughters were growing up.

The three sisters lived far away from each other after they left home, until recently; but whenever one of them was in need, the other two would manage to be there for support. Candace's first illness was what brought the idea of living near each other to fulfillment. The other two sisters realized that they were no longer happy to pay each other visits during emergencies and holidays, but wanted to be able to participate in each other's lives daily. After Candace got well, they talked about "the healing power of family." They decided they could no longer afford to wait until someone was ill to call the family together; they had come to believe that being together was part of their ongoing health.

"Health isn't just physical," Angela's mom had concluded. "It's mental and spiritual. Each one of us contributes as a part to complete the whole family."

After Grandma Heather and Grandpop moved to a condo in Emerald Circle Valley, Amma Brenna and Grandpa Jack were the only holdouts to this plan. "I lived in the frozen north long enough," declared Amma. "Our farm is within a day's driving distance, so we can be there when we want—during warm weather hopefully!" Amma

111

was convinced that since she'd grown up in the cold of Iceland's long, sunless winters, she was reaping a well-deserved respite in her "golden years" on her beloved pony farm in sunny Tennessee. She didn't mind coming north for the Christmas holidays because "there should be snow at Christmas." She bustled in the door bringing an arsenal of fireworks for Christmas and New Year's Eve because that was the Icelandic tradition. The rest of the winter, she held court at her home outside the Snow Belt, inviting everyone to visit and "warm up before spring." They all had to admit it was nice to be able to leave the gray slush behind for holidays like Valentine's Day and Easter when they could get away.

But today Angela was glad at least one grandmother could be there with her aunts and mom. Grandma Heather looked up as they entered the waiting room and opened her arms. In all the eggshell colors of the sterile hospital, here was a ray of sunlight. Bren ran to her first and hugged her, burying his head on her ample shoulder. He cried and felt comforted by her calm love. Grandpop put an arm around both their shoulders.

112

23

Escaping Light

"HOW IS SHE?" Angela sat down next to her mom on the hard pleather of the turquoise couch.

Mom answered in a low voice to avoid attracting the attention of Cara and Heather, who were mesmerized by a kiddy show on the large-screen TV in the corner. "We don't know yet. The doctors gave her something to make her more comfortable, but they don't know what is causing the pain. She seems weaker than she did before they gave her anything, but at least she isn't hurting."

"Is Thomas coming?"

"He's looking for a plane ticket that will get him here in a couple of days, then he can cancel if they find out it's something that's not serious, like indigestion or the flu. The tour is over in two weeks, so after that he'll be home for quite a while. We are going to call him as soon as we hear from her doctor."

Aunt Chloe opened the door to the waiting room and looked around. "Angela, you're here. Candace said you could come back to her room when you got here if you want to. They're only allowing one person with her at a time, and she wants you to see for yourself that she's okay."

It was a lonely walk to find Aunt Candace. Angela followed the nurse's white lab coat. Everything was too white, too bright, and too reflective in this polished chrome-and-glass world. There were no nature smells or sounds. The racket of intercoms made everyone's voice sound robotic. Poor Aunt Candace! This was not like home at all. The nurse opened a door for Angela and smiled a weak smile, like she was drained of her emotion just as much as the hospital was drained of color.

Angela peeked into the room before entering to make sure she wasn't disturbing anyone. Suddenly a burst of color that was like a little sparkler on a cloudy night met her eyes. Aunt Candace sat propped up in the hospital bed, the white hospital linens covered with a fleece blanket that was printed with a riot of fall-color leaf patterns and decorated with green featherstitching around the edges. Her bright red hair was fluffed up like dozens of little candle flames, and she was wearing a cool green robe. Mom and Chloe must have been at work the minute they got there. A big vase of sunflowers posed gracefully on the little nightstand. Several colorful crayon drawings had already been taped up on the walls, signed in large letters by Cara and Heather. As soon as Angela stepped in, a camera flash went off, momentarily blinding her.

"Now there's a look of surprise," Aunt Candace chuckled. "You weren't expecting to get your photo taken just now, were you?"

"Cute, Aunt Candace," Angela said, recovering as a camera flash spot danced around her field of vision. "That's payback for the scare I gave you the other night, huh?"

"Well, surprise photos were your suggestion," Candace smiled as she accepted her niece's hug. Angela was relieved to see her aunt was feeling well enough to tease her, but she thought the hug felt a little weak.

"How are you?" She gave Candace a "tell me the truth" look.

"I'm sleepy from some pain medicine, but I feel okay. I'm breathing more easily now." Angela noticed there was a clear plastic oxygen line running under her nose. Aunt Candace made fun of it as she laid her head back into the pillow. "It's like a little nose fan. Very refreshing."

"Oh, I see. So you're just taking it easy like you're at a spa or something," Angela said, taking the bait of reassurance to make her aunt feel at ease. She didn't want Candace wearing herself out just to prove that she really was as "okay" as she claimed.

"Yes, yes. I have it pretty easy here. I'm just loitering in bed being waited on until they tell me I can go home.

It's hard to keep a sunbeam down . . . you know. Hmmm. I was just giving a talk about that when I had to come here."

"About sunbeams?"

"Yes, and how hard we have to work as photographers to keep our darkrooms 'light tight.' You know stray beams of light are the photo printer's worst problem. Light penetrates any tiny crack in your darkroom door or the lid of your camera. You have to control light if you want nice sharp prints—even the tiniest beam is so powerful that you have to be on constant alert to keep it out while you are making them. People get afraid of the darkness, but if they knew how fragile it is when compared with light, they would laugh. When I open the lid of a black 'light-tight' canister, the light leaps in and illuminates every corner. The darkness doesn't come creeping out trying to get you—it's just vanquished. It's completely destroyed—immediately! Light is the greatest force there is. That's why Jesus called himself 'The Light of the World,' I think."

"I like that," Angela said. "You'll have to give me the whole lecture sometime. Right now, I was told not to tire you, so maybe I'll do the talking, and you can just lie back there and relax."

"That's fine, dear," Aunt Candace said cooperatively. "How about telling me about your day? Any good stories or newsy tidbits I should know about?"

"Uh, not really. Boring day at school as usual. Why don't I read you something? I see a stack of books and magazines here. Look at this, there's some new photo editing software described in this magazine. Want to hear about it?" Angela thought her day might be a little too exciting for Candace. She'd surely be concerned about Marti if Angela told her about Clay. She began to read all the technical information about the software program, and Candace's eyes started to close. Soon she was asleep. The painkiller probably made her relaxed enough to nap.

Angela looked at her watch and decided to go back to the waiting room and see if anyone else wanted to see Aunt Candace. She looked so peaceful sleeping there under the bright blanket. Maybe nothing was seriously wrong after all.

When she got back to where the family was sitting, they all looked at her for the news. "She's sleeping now," Angela told them.

"I think she was keeping herself awake because she knew you were coming," Mom said. "Now she can have a good long rest. I'll sit with her to make sure someone is there when she wakes up," Grandma Heather said, rising from the couch.

"We can take turns doing that tonight if you men want to go home for dinner and get the little girls in bed," Chloe said.

"Mike and I can make hamburgers," Dad offered.

"No problem," Mike grinned. Chloe gave him a warning look, but didn't comment.

The little girls were thrilled to see Angela, once their attention was wrested from the TV. Bren took a minute to go to Candace's room with Grandma and look inside to see her peacefully sleeping. With that done, he was satisfied that she was in good hands, and he walked to the cars with Grandpa and the others.

They left the Land Rover for the ladies and drove home in Mike's, Dad's, and Grandpop's cars. "So let's make some nice, juicy burgers, guys," Mike chuckled. Everyone knew what that meant. They were going to drive through Biggie Burgers. Mike reviewed some fancy restaurants for his job, but he loved what he called Biggie's "lowdown-no-good-greaseburgers" as a change of pace. To be fair, Biggie probably used the least greasy hamburger money could buy. They were just juicy and messy. He also made kid-size mini-burgers and tiny fries that the girls loved.

The men caravanned through the drive-thru and came away with burgers, fries, onion rings, and milkshakes. They spread it all out on the kitchen table and chowed down together. And no one was home to scold them about it not being health food!

"Here, let me do the dishes," Grandpop said. He scooped up all the paper wrappers and threw them in the trash. Just then the phone rang, and he picked it up. "Yes, we're through with dinner. Uh-huh, Mike gave us burgers . . . right, that was quick. Here, I'll let him tell you."

He gave the phone to Mike, rolling his eyes in warning.

"Hi, honey. Yes, they ate all their dinner. Vegetables? Potatoes and lettuce. Uh, not exactly a salad . . . okay. Bye." He turned to the kids and gave the orders. "The moms say baths and bed for you two. Stable work, homework, showers, and bed for you two. Let's go."

The little girls went with Mike. Bren and Angela went to the barn to feed and bed down the horses for the night.

Dad followed to check on Bobcat's leg, and Grandpop went along with him.

"So what was Chloe asking you about on the phone?" Dad chuckled. "Sounded like you almost gave us up about the Biggie Burgers!"

Grandpop laughed back, "Something tells me I didn't have to—she really sounded suspicious. I think Mike's in trouble. Man, that girl is strict! She takes after her mom—a spitfire, as my dad used to say! Now, what did you start to tell me is going on with the little Arabian pony?"

"Just a strain, I think. A little rest should take care of it. He's a beauty, though. You've seen him before with Angela's friend riding. Just thought you'd like a look up close," Dad said.

Angela thought they must have left the barn light on because she could see it as they neared the door. They probably wouldn't have noticed it in the morning light, but as the daylight was waning, its glow was now visible. She pulled open the door and was startled to see someone standing inside. It was Marti.

119

24

Secrets

MARTI'S HAND was on Bobcat's nose. She looked just as startled as Angela. But there was another look there—like she was feeling guilty. She almost looked like she was about to run away—if there had been a back door she could have run out of.

"Uh, hi, Angela . . . I, uh, just wanted to see how Bobcat is. That's okay, isn't it?"

"Well, of course, silly, he's your horse. My barn is your barn, right? I'm sorry I didn't meet you after school. My dad picked me up early."

Maybe Marti felt uncomfortable because I wasn't there and wondered if something was wrong, Angela thought.

But it didn't sound like that was it, because Marti answered with, "Oh . . . oh, yeah. Actually, I went straight home and forgot to look for you. But later I thought you might be here. I was just going to go up to the house to get you." Why did that sound like a lie? Bren was looking at Marti as if something was weird, too. He turned to Angela with a question in his eyes.

At that moment Dad and Grandpop caught up to them. "Well, speak of the devil, there's our Marti. How are you feeling today?" Dad asked.

"Fine, Mr. Clarkson," she answered uneasily. "I was just stopping by to see how Bobcat is feeling. And I got him a crystal headstall for his halter. It's supposed to make him feel calmer."

Marti had added a shiny beaded cover to the top of Bobcat's green nylon halter. It looked a little too fancy for daily use, like a tiara at a picnic. Everyone smiled at it, and Grandpop said Bobcat looked "princely."

Dad had Marti take the pony out into the corral and walk him around. By this time, Roy Rogers had come up from the back of the pasture to greet his people. "I think you can put Roy back in his stall for the night," Dad said. "Bobcat is improved, but I don't think he's ready to ride home yet. He can share Sammy's stall. There's plenty of room for two ponies in a twelve-by-twelve stall. I'll rewrap his leg for extra protection after he stretches it a little here. Marti, would you walk him around a few more minutes while Bren and Angela clean the stalls?"

They got busy mucking out the two stalls, but when everyone else was outside, Bren whispered to Angela,

121

"What was going on with Marti? She acted like she'd gotten caught or something . . . she wasn't doing anything wrong, was she?"

Angela shrugged. So she wasn't imagining it. Little kids were hard to fool. She had the same respect for children's intuition that she did for Roy's sixth sense on trails. What had been going on? The only time she'd seen Marti look like that was when she caught her trying a cigarette with some other girls in the restroom at school once. But she didn't smell any smoke in the barn, and Marti would never smoke there for sure. It was one of the most dangerous things you could do in a barn, with all the hay and dry wood around. Every year they'd hear of a barn fire and horses injured somewhere because someone had been careless with smokes. That wasn't it.

122

"So do you need a ride home, or is your mom coming to get you?" Dad asked Marti after they'd put the horses away and headed back to the house.

"She'll come to get me if I call," Marti replied.

"Well, we're going back to the hospital to let Mom, Chloe, and Grandma come home for a while," Dad said. "We can save her a trip since she's already driven over here once. Why don't you give her a call and let her know she can relax?"

"Sure, thanks a lot," Marti replied. There it was again—that funny look like she was hiding something.

Angela decided she'd better talk to her friend alone and find out what was really going on. Marti was terrible at lying. She'd get the truth out of her. They went upstairs together while the guys got drinks from the fridge.

"Okay, what is up?" Angela said as soon as they got to her room. "Why didn't you want to call your mom, and what are you looking so guilty about?"

"Well, my mom doesn't actually know where I am," Marti began. "She thinks I'm at the library."

"Well, if your mom didn't bring you over here, who did?"

"Uh, I guess I'd have to say Clay gave me a ride," Marti giggled.

"What? And does your mom know about him?"

"Well, she knows about him in a general sense—she hasn't met him yet," Marti said, then added, "but he wants to meet her."

Dad called from the bottom of the stairs, "Marti, we're just about ready to go."

"Coming, Mr. Clarkson," she answered. "Listen, Angela, I've got to go, but don't worry about me. I've got horse sense, remember? I'm NOT going to end up like Kelly or Jill. I'll always be a horsewoman first, and I'll find a way to ride with you again. Clay wants the best for me, and he is believing with me that I won't have to sell Bobcat and my parents will stay together."

"I hope that comes true," Angela said, giving her a hug good-bye.

"I know it will. Here, Clay gave me something for you, too. He said it would keep us together if we both have one." Marti held up another crystal on a necklace like her own and pressed it into Angela's hand.

Angela looked at it as her friend bounded down the stairs. What was this guy Clay, a jeweler? She held the gem up to her desk light. The crystal was clear, but had a silvery tint. In the middle of it she could see some metallic specks suspended together in a funny shape. It almost looked like the figure of a person flying or swimming in the middle of the crystal.

As she was looking at it, Bren came up the stairs. Cara was following him. "Goodnight, Angela," she said sweetly. This was one of her favorite bedtime stalling ploys. It took a while for her to climb the stairs and then go back down to bed. Angela looked at her—so sweet, and yet so crafty at such a young age. She hated to reward her for playing her dad like this, but if he let her go, it was his own fault. She gave the little trickster a kiss and told her firmly to go back to her daddy. She could see Cara knew she'd been caught. Yet, she had one more ploy and that was to ask Angela about something that would take up some more time in the telling. It could be anything, from Angela's hairstyle to her horses. "Oh, pretty," she said as she saw the necklace. "Can I hold it? Where did you get it?"

"What is that?" Bren asked. Angela handed it to him first. "Wow, that's a nice quartz crystal! Hey, it's got a phantom in it, too."

"What's that?" Angela asked.

"It's another mineral in the middle of the crystal. Crystals start out small and grow, almost as if they were plants instead of rocks. If they grow around another small rock, it becomes part of the crystal. It looks like silver or . . . hmmm. This crystal swings toward my metal belt buckle when I hold it near. Maybe it's got magnetite in the middle. Cool! Look, it swings the other way if I move it. That's got to be what's in there. Magnetite is magnetic."

"Can I have one?" Cara asked.

"I'll give it to you if you go right back to your dad now," Angela coaxed. She didn't care about having a crystal that looked just like Marti's, especially since it came from Clay. She was tired of hearing about him and his jewelry and his weird philosophy.

Cara was perfectly happy to take the pretty prize and go to bed. She skipped off with the necklace around her neck to show her dad and sister.

"You worried about this crystal stuff?" Bren asked his sister, noticing her expression.

"Kind of. I'm not really worried about it being true or anything; it's just that I think Marti is taking it too seriously, and she's probably going to get her heart broken in the end. She needs something to cling to for hope right now and I just wish she'd chosen to have faith in something more . . ."

"Real?"

Angela looked at her brother a second. Bren had the most sincere face in the world. And he had such a pure and simple faith in God. She remembered when the world was more black and white like that for her. Years ago. "Maybe that's it. Not that crystals aren't real. You can touch them and wear them. A lot of people think they are special."

Now Bren put on his "little scientist" face. "Well, they might be special, but they aren't exactly rare here. There are crystals all over the place in the kind of clay we have. I've found them by our barn and along the trails. You don't have to dig very deep to find a clump of them. The guys and I collected a whole box of them to use for pirate treasure last summer. Our earth science book says they have a lot of interesting uses, but I don't see why anyone would have faith in them."

"What kind of things did your book say crystals are used for?"

"They have something called 'resonance' that makes them vibrate when electricity goes through them, so people use them in some watches and in radio transmitters. Because of a crystal's shape it can bend light that goes through it, so it can be used to focus light where you want it or to split it into a rainbow. There are all kinds of machines and experiments that use light through crystals."

126

Angela smiled as she listened. Bren was an interesting little guy, playing pirate and scientist with the same toy. She wondered what he'd be like when he grew up.

25

Another Crystal

THE BIG NEWS the next morning was that Thomas would be arriving in two days to stay home for the rest of the concert series. He felt he'd be justified in leaving the tour early even if Candace's illness turned out to be nothing serious. He told Dad what he'd told his conductor: "You just don't let your true love sit around alone in the hospital if there's a way you can be there. If it's possible my being there next to her might give her the strength to get better, then I should be there." Well, it was a strong enough argument to convince everyone, and his understudy was eager to fill in, so he would be on his way home after tonight's concert, which just happened to be at the Paris Opera House—the beautiful old building where he and Candace had met.

The thought of his coming did seem to help Candace right away. She ate her breakfast well and seemed much stronger afterward. Angela and Grandma Heather drove over to sit with her so the others could go home for some rest. Sit and wait was all the doctors had given them to do. They weren't ready to say what they'd found from her tests—if they'd found anything.

Angela and Grandma Heather brought a bag with books and other items Candace had requested. "If I have to sit here and wait, I might as well catch up on my reading or my scrapbooking, especially since my mom's here to help me!"

Grandma Heather was the master scrapbooker of the family—she'd been creating her own custom albums since before they were a trendy thing to do. She liked to write funny sayings or cute poems next to the pictures. On some pages, she'd insert the recipes for a holiday meal or special cake Amma Brenna had created that was shown in the family photo for that page.

They started going over Candace's plan for completing an album of old photos, spreading out pictures, little souvenir items, and stickers across the bedcovers and on the nightstand. It was a great diversion for Candace for a while, but she soon looked tired, and they decided to just look through the photos and chat about them.

Grandma Heather collected the scrapping material and put it away. She looked like an older version of Candace, more so than she did the other sisters, but it seemed like each of the three had inherited a part of her

128

talent—if talent is really inherited. Chloe loved cooking, Claire made her living writing, and Candace loved photography. Maybe she just taught them to do the things she knew best. They certainly got their love of the Bible from her. She'd say, "Listen up now, this big book is not just for pressing flowers—you will find life if you search the Scriptures." However, Grandma would be the first to admit that her Bibles were full of pressed flowers that ultimately ended up in her albums or on her handmade greeting cards.

They talked about their family and the "little red hens" growing up as they looked at old photos. Years ago, it was popular to color black and white photos by hand when the client wanted a fancy portrait to frame. It made them look like oil paintings. Grandma Heather was one of the last of the artists who did this for a living. Grandpop took the photos and printed them on canvas board, and then she colored them with paint. It was a special memory for Candace.

"I used to sit next to her on the bed and watch her hand-paint the blush on people's cheeks or swirl in their hair color. She had a description of the shade of lipstick they wore or what color their eyes were. She used to tease me because I wanted to watch and she'd say, 'Okay, but you have to sit still. Don't shake the bed.' Then she'd make little warning noises if I started to wiggle. I must have looked funny trying to sit perfectly still. The paint smell made my nose itch, and I used to twitch it around, so I didn't have to move my hand to scratch it. She'd finally end up laughing, if I didn't sneeze or something first. I didn't realize she had been amusing herself at my expense until I was older. I think Mom and Dad entertained themselves with us 'three little red hens' all the time, but we didn't get the jokes until we grew up."

"Oh, you poor thing! You really suffered," grinned Grandma Heather.

Chloe and her girls loved to go to Grandma Heather's and cook with her. Chloe found it a challenge to keep up with what her mom was tossing into a recipe, especially since Grandma liked to improvise. If she was short on an ingredient, she might adjust the whole recipe or substitute something completely different. On the inspiration of the moment, she might add something entirely new. She also tended to measure with her cupped hands instead of using measuring utensils, so it sometimes looked like she was just tossing clouds of flour everywhere. That made it hard for Chloe to write down exact amounts. Grandma Heather also had secret ingredients in some recipes that she was reluctant to give up information about. "Just taste it, you'll figure out what it is," she'd tease. It drove Chloe crazy.

Something else was driving Angela crazy that day. When they'd gotten to Candace's room, she noticed that there was a new addition to the decorations. Another one of Marti's necklaces was hanging above the bed, reflecting the electric ceiling light like a sun catcher. Candace noticed her looking at it again and said, "Oh, your friend Marti sent that over with your dad. Pretty, isn't it? Wasn't that nice of her?"

Angela couldn't decide if it was "nice" or if Marti's fanaticism was now becoming fully annoying. She was starting to really push this thing on people. That was weird for Marti because she had always said she hated it when people "pushed religion" on her. *Now this crystal thing seems to be growing into something more religious than decorative,* Angela thought. She didn't want to upset Aunt Candace now that she was feeling better, so she decided to wait for a chance to talk to Grandma alone. She knew her aunt would have all kinds of questions about Clay and want to talk to the other sisters about it. Maybe they'd all decide to talk to Marti's mom and cause her friend to get angry about the intrusion or think Angela had betrayed her by talking to them about it.

Angela both loved and loathed her aunts' lively interest in her life and how it extended into the lives of her friends. Marti thought that the "little red hens" were cute and said Angela was lucky to have such a close family. Angela understood why this was such a sweet picture to an outsider. She loved the sisters when they were busy with their own things and amusing themselves with their own stories. She just didn't want her life to become the center of their discussions. Sometimes, especially since she'd become a teenager, it felt like every little pebble of information she tossed their way created such a giant splash that the ripples of conversation about it would never end.

Luckily, Aunt Candace brought up a safer subject. "Look at what a good sun catcher that crystal is—making rainbows all over the walls, even though we don't have a window in here," she smiled. "You know the rainbow is a sign of God's promise to save us from harm. Isn't it amazing that an ordinary beam of light contains so many colors that we can't see unless they are broken through a prism?"

"I always think about that when a rainbow comes after a big thunderstorm," Grandma said. "We don't recognize the beauty surrounding us in everyday things like sunshine until after some dark clouds and a good drenching take them away temporarily and remind us how much we were enjoying them."

"I guess I do take a lot for granted," Angela agreed. "Like you, Aunt Candace. I expected to see you at the breakfast table this morning like every day. I missed your sunshine!"

Normally Aunt Candace would have given Angela a hug after a sentimental comment like that. Today she just reached over and squeezed Angela's hand and gave her such a big smile it crinkled her nose. *Not quite feeling all better*, Angela thought. Maybe it was still the medication making her feel weak.

A nurse tapped on the door and announced that she needed to take Candace to the lab for some more tests. "It's after noon. You two ladies might want to get a sandwich or take a walk. This will take at least an hour," she informed them.

"Yes, you run along," Aunt Candace encouraged. "I'll probably be tired when I get back and want a nap."

As they left, Grandma kissed her daughter on the forehead as if she were still her little girl. Angela had the startling thought that moms might never stop thinking of their children as "children," even when they are completely and utterly grown up. "Will my mom still be kissing me on the forehead when I'm forty-five?" she asked her Grandma after they walked into the hallway.

"Why? Is that such a scary thought?" Grandma asked. "Don't you think it's still a comfort to be looked after once you've become all grown up?"

"I'm already annoyed with it sometimes," she confessed. "I can't imagine how much worse it would be at Candace's age. Don't moms ever stop thinking of us as their little kids?"

"Well, it's hard to get those cute pictures out of your mind after all the years of reading stories or sitting at a child's bedside when they're sick . . . It's not that we don't think our children have become perfectly competent adults; it's just that we have beautiful loving memories. And when we want to comfort our children, we want them to remember how it was, too, and to realize that we are still here for them as much today as we were yesterday. Isn't that okay?"

Angela looked at her grandma's sweet face with all its laugh lines and freckles. She felt a little embarrassed and thought it might have sounded like she was whining. "Of course, I just . . ."

Grandma laughed and put an arm around her shoulder. "You don't have to explain, honey. I was just teasing you a little. I understand. That sort of thing can be way too mushy for someone your age. You might change your mind about it later."

133

26

Changes

S O YOU CHANGED your mind about a lot of things
when you grew up, huh?" Angela said. They
rounded the corner into the little coffee shop
that was part of the hospital lobby. Angela liked this part
of the building much better. The weathered red brick
walls felt cozy and the floor was made of old varnished
wood that didn't make footsteps sound as menacing as
the marble floors in the rest of the place. They sat down
in a booth next to a brass plaque that marked the original cornerstone of the building with "1859" engraved
in fancy numerals. Under the date, a notation said the
original building had been a flourmill. Angela looked
at the date and realized that stone had been there
before her grandmother was born. She touched the old
stone and thought that the whole world had changed

since this stone was placed. "I can't imagine getting old," she said.

"Well, you sound so sad about it! Maybe growing up isn't like you think," her grandmother smiled. "I don't feel any older today than I did when I got my first driver's license. I get surprised almost every time I look in the mirror. I think, *Is that my grandmother in there?* and I have to remember that I'm over sixty-five. Or when I see a pair of roller skates at the store and want to buy them for myself, I have to remember that I might fall and break a hip or something. So I buy them for you or for Brendan. You know, I think I have just as good a time watching you ride horses as if I were riding myself."

Angela could not imagine watching anything ever being as fun as doing it. As if Grandma could tell what she was thinking, she said, "I think it's because after you do something so many times, you know exactly how it feels. You know how it feels when you sail over a three-foot jump and your timing is right in sync with your horse. Do it enough times over forty years, and you'll feel every muscle stretch and bend when you watch someone else do it. At least that's my theory. I really do get as much fun watching you do it—and I don't get muddy!"

Angela realized her sweet little granny was now ribbing her about the last time she watched her practice jumping. She had just been working Roy over a few easy jumps and had decided to ride bareback because the sun was so hot. She'd gotten a little careless and didn't slow him down over the last jump. He took it before she was set, and she slid right off his side and into a patch of muck. Angela laughed remembering how dumb she'd felt in front of her grandparents. "Another member of the upside-down club," Grandma had chided when she saw her grandchild was unharmed.

Now she said, "It gets a lot more difficult to pick yourself up from those upside-down club meetings after you pass forty. I think the ground gets harder or something. I know the mud is less and less appealing. I've never even liked the mud packs they smear on you at the spas."

"That really *is* a gross idea," Angela laughed. "Although my friend Teri went to a spa where they gave her a chocolate facial. She said it tasted great, and her skin was really soft afterwards. Maybe I will change my mind about lots of things when I'm old. I've already changed the way I look at life a lot since I was a little kid like Cara or Bren.

"When I was Bren's age I just plain believed in God. Something's happened to my brain or my spirit over the last few years. The way I used to believe everything the Bible says or whatever Mom and Dad believe isn't working for me anymore."

"Well, of course not," said Grandma. "The faith you had as a child doesn't fit you anymore, just like your first riding boots don't fit. You have to move up to the next size, and then the next, as you grow. You can't keep on taking other people's word for it about faith when you are growing up. You have to find your own."

"Hmmm . . . that sounds a lot nicer of a thing to say

than it is to do," Angela said, trying to keep her voice from sounding like she was whining about it. "I've taken comparative religion class in school, and it didn't help me decide anything. All it did was confuse me. All the religions sound like they have good intentions and make their followers into better people. But they contradict each other. They can't all be right."

"Yes, I guess that would be a difficult way to try and decide your spiritual path! It's like going through a book about all the breeds of horses and trying to decide which is best. You know you are a rider, and they are all horses! Is any one really better than another?"

They ordered soup and sandwiches from the menu. The server brought them iced tea, and Grandma asked Angela another question as they sipped their drinks. "How did you ever decide on your mustang, may I ask?"

"Oh, I didn't really pick Roy. It was more like he picked me," Angela said. "I wasn't really looking to get a new horse when I met him, even though I knew I'd have to have one eventually—or get elevator horseshoes put on Sammy so my feet wouldn't drag the ground! One day I was helping Dad at a barn where they were bringing in some mustangs to gentle and sell as pets. I could see Roy was different, even though he was a mess. He wouldn't let anyone near him until I started talking to him through the fence. Then he just came up to me like he already knew me and coaxed me to get to know him. I couldn't resist."

"So then you jumped on the back of this wild horse who'd never been ridden, and everything went just fine?"

Grandma asked.

"Oh, no, of course not," Angela laughed. "The first time I got on him, he bolted and took off out of the fence and into the field. All I could do was hold on until he got tired and stopped. We had a few wild rides before we worked out our communication. We had to learn to trust each other."

"Hmmm, that's interesting. So it was more about relationship than research?"

"Are you saying that's what it's like with God?" Angela asked suspiciously. "I've heard that from Mom and the aunts. They talk like God will just call out my name, and I'll hear it—I've never heard anything so far, and I've asked him to talk to me."

"Well, did Roy call out your name to get you to come over to the fence?" Grandma asked.

"No, but he let me know I was invited, the way horses do," she answered.

"Well, God communicates with us the way he does, too. And it's usually different from the way we talk with each other. You had to learn the subtle way horses communicate to know Roy was inviting you. I think it's the same with God. He invites us in his own special way. It's different for different people. I think he knows the way each person will understand best. You just have to stick around and be listening for it," Grandma said.

The server brought their soup and some grilled sandwiches. Grandma took Angela's hand and then quietly prayed a blessing as she always did, whether they were at home or at a restaurant:

"Dear Lord, thank you for this food. Bless it to our use and bless the hands that prepared it. Speak to my lovely granddaughter in the way she will understand it best. In Jesus' name I pray. Amen."

For once Angela didn't look around to see if the server or other diners were looking at them while they were praying. She prayed silently along with Grandma, "Yes, God. I'm ready to hear from you. Show me how to know you better. Forgive me for all my doubts and complaining."

"You know," Grandma continued, "some people listen to God by reading the Bible, others by prayer or just stillness. You always can ask him to talk to you in a way you'll understand. Trust me, he's more anxious to talk to you than you are to hear him if you are like most of us."

This was news to Angela. She had always felt it was her obligation to seek out God or a guru of some kind who'd give her the answers. Maybe the answers were already there, and she'd ignored them, thinking they were just her own thoughts. Was God already talking to her?

139

27

Visiting Hours

I T WAS A LONG day with Grandma and Aunt Candace, and at the end of it they still had only vague answers from the doctors about what was wrong. The worry on her grandmother's face was starting to set in frown wrinkles that were seldom seen, and Aunt Candace's eyes darted nervously toward the door whenever a nurse knocked. Angela wished Thomas could get there sooner. She was relieved when her mom came to pick them up, and they left Candace sleeping fitfully in the dim light of her little room. She'd insisted everyone go home and get some rest, since she was no longer in any pain.

Candace was actually glad to be alone for a bit, to not see the worry in everyone's eyes or hear that concerned undertone in everything they said. She wished she could be at the Paris Opera House with Thomas. He should be finishing the concert soon. She pictured her beloved husband trying to get his tuxedo to button right and tie his tie by himself. He became even more silent and stoic when he was full of nervous energy before a performance. She imagined the intense expression on his handsome face and sighed.

The old opera house was a wonderful place, full of history and tradition. Candace would always remember entering the front door for the first time. The "mistral" wind had been blowing for days, so to keep her head warm she had worn a cute wool hat that she found at a tiny boutique called "Penelope." As she walked up the marble stairs, a stronger than usual gust of air actually blew the hat off her head. She reached up and caught it as it flew away and found herself staring into the laughing face of a sculpture of a dancing angel. His perfect white arms were raised as if he had just knocked off her little hat. The ivory face held an expression that was such a mix of joy and mischief that she had laughed out loud at his prank.

She stared at the little crystal reflecting the dim nightlight that was the room's only illumination. She lifted it off the metal frame above her bed and let it dangle from its chain, twirling around and around. Rainbows danced across the walls making sparkles on the dull beige paint. She began to hear music from far away and wondered if someone in the next room had turned on the TV. The music almost sounded like the ending to a new piece Thomas had been practicing before he left. The little rainbows danced in time to the sound, moving apart,

141

then together. It looked as if they were drawing a curtain away from the wall—like a theatre curtain now that she looked again. She started to sit up to get a better view, and then she suddenly gasped and reached out her hand toward the wall. There on the other side of the parted curtain stood Thomas. He was playing with the orchestra. Candace stood up next to the bed and noticed that little swirls of fog were forming at her feet. Bizarre! She began to walk toward her husband and the gray swirls parted as she stepped into them.

When Angela got home, she went into the library to do the assignments she'd brought from school earlier. Kyle was supposed to stop by and drop off the day's homework as well as notes from the classes they had together. Angela looked out over the wide view of the Emerald Circle Valley and admired the sunset and all the little lights winking on from the houses below. The village had been named for the circle of six green hills that surrounded it like jewels on a necklace. The farmhouse sat on one of the hills, so you could see the other hills and a sweeping view of the valley from the library. The hospital sat on another of the hills directly across the valley. The hill next to it was where the high school was built, and Angela could see the lights from the football field. Football and marching band practice would soon be finishing up there. The road sloped from the school into the town center on the far side of the bowl of the valley, and she could see how the shine from its sleepy streetlights mingled into a milky glow. On the near side of the valley a lower indentation that was slightly darker than the rest marked where the secret trail from Marti's house dipped down to the creek bed and the abandoned cottage. Marti's house had been built on the hill nearest to that part of the valley, so Angela could see the top of her roof beyond the ridge of trees. Seeing it reminded her that she ought to call Marti as soon as she was done with her homework. Bren had offered to bed down the horses for the night, so Angela had no excuse for not getting started.

Just as she was unloading her book bag, Cara came skipping through the library holding a black toy horse in front of her. "What are you doing, Angela? Want to play with my horses?" she asked.

"Sorry, sweetie," Angela said. "I have to do my homework now."

"Okay. I have to feed my Bobcat and put him to bed . . ." Cara said and continued skipping her horse out of the room.

Angela glanced up from her work and thought she could see the little headlight from Kyle's minibike winding up her hill from the valley road. She was glad it was Kyle who volunteered to help her. He took the most detailed notes of all her friends and although the way he'd bring up little "factoids" he'd picked up from a lecture was sometimes irritating to listen to at lunch, there were times this attention to detail came in handy—and this was one of those times. He had an uncanny talent for guessing which tidbits of information would be included on tests. Angela thought she'd seen teachers looking Kyle's way to see if he was writing down a note as they threw an obscure kibble into the lecture. Madame Corbeau designated those random questions "for the perspicacious among you." Angela opened her French workbook. If she finished filling in the blanks before Kyle got there, she could tear out the worksheets and send them back with him. She scribbled hastily as the sun made its final exit behind the western hill, and the Chalice Moon took over the night sky.

The doorbell rang, and Chloe called out, "Angelaaah, Kyle's here," as she walked him to the library. Filling in the last question on the worksheet, Angela began to tear it out as she heard their footsteps outside the doorway. "Have you seen Cara?" Chloe asked with a frown as they entered the library.

"She came through here earlier. She's probably trying to get busy with something that will put off bedtime," Angela said knowingly.

"That little sneak—discipline has gone downhill with Daddy in charge for two days. Cara and Heather can wrap him around their little finger," Chloe complained.

"You know, I think I saw her in the flower garden as I came in," said Kyle. "She did look like she was hiding or something."

"Oh, great. That's too much. Ca-a-ara!" Chloe yelled as she walked away. Cara was in for it.

"Tattletale," Angela accused.

"What?" exclaimed Kyle with a startled look. "Was I supposed to let a little kid run around in the dark all alone?"

"No, you did the right thing—of course," she teased.

"Oh, so you think I'm a brownnose now! That's the thanks I get for lugging your homework up the hill and almost freezing to death on my bike? It's really windy out there and . . ."

"Here, have a cookie," Angela said stopping him mid-whine by holding out a plate of chocolate and peanut butter squares Chloe had baked earlier.

"That'll do," Kyle smiled, taking the plate and handing over Angela's assignment folder.

"Madame Corbeau says to tell your Aunt Candace she'll be praying for her. How do they know each other?"

"Oh, Aunt Candace came to class and gave a slideshow on Paris once. Apparently, Madame Corbeau had seen the photo book she did about touring France with the orchestra."

"Ha! Who's the brownie now?" Kyle grinned. "I bet you got some points for that . . ."

"Okay, I'm probably brownier-than-thou. Let's drop it. What's new from the lunch room?" she asked.

Kyle's eyes sparkled waiting for that question. "You are not going to believe what happened today," he began.

145

28

Kyle

K YLE SAT DOWN on the comfy couch and put his feet up on the ottoman. For once he had some news that Angela hadn't heard yet.

"Tell me already," she said. What was he doing, making a game of making her wait? That was exactly what he was doing.

"Well, okay. Today Simone made first chair in the saxophone section. That's right! She finally got up the guts to challenge Lex Gerkin for it." Kyle crossed his arms with satisfaction at Angela's reaction.

"What? Lex is a senior! That's amazing! So, Simone is in charge of the sax section now?" Angela exclaimed.

"She is! And you know Simone; she's a dictator at heart. Today the sax section—tomorrow the world!

Michelle, Adam, and Teri were already calling her 'Master' at lunch."

"No doubt that is an amazing thing—a sophomore getting to be in charge of upperclassmen. She must be glowing," said Angela.

"Glowering is more like it. She's already complaining about the 'lack of discipline' in her section. You should hear it."

Angela laughed aloud, "I can hear it already!" Simone was a tiny terror. The petite brunette had dimples all over her heart-shaped face when she smiled, but make her mad and she could throw a look that would turn you to stone. "Next thing, she'll be lobbying to become drum major."

"Oh, yeah. She wants to get ahold of that bullhorn, alright," Kyle said, rolling his eyes. "I can just see her on the platform with Mr. Sandler yelling, 'Straighten those lines! Don't make me come down there!'"

Angela started laughing so hard she almost choked on her cookie. Next to herself, Kyle was the best imaginer of their group. She could always tell when he had been mentally projecting the "logical conclusion" of something the rest of them were talking about. He'd get a certain smirk at the corners of his mouth, and later Angela would ask what it was about. They'd probably never want to tell Simone about their comic projection of her, but it would give the two of them some funny inside jokes as she fulfilled their predictions.

147

In a minute, Kyle stood up and shook off the laugh. "Wow, your house has got the best view of the valley there is . . . I can see all six hills from here. Did you ever hear the story about them being part of the Underground Railroad?"

"I heard something about it. We've got some writing on the cornerstone in the barn that looks like a map in some sort of code."

Kyle looked interested. "I'd like to see it sometime. They say each of the six hills has a hiding place and the 'train conductors' used to spirit the runaway slaves from one hill to another when bounty hunters came looking for them. According to legend there was also supposed to be a secret exit that led to the next town in the railroad, but the historical society is still trying to find information about that. There are references that suggest it could even be a tunnel. All they've come up with is that locating the exit path had something to do with the alignment of the Big Dipper and the six hills."

They were silent for a moment as they looked out the picture window. They thought about the long years the hills and trees spread out before them had been there. The Big Dipper swung low on the horizon and the Chalice Moon had tipped to one side as if to pour its crimson contents into the dipper cup.

Kyle cleared his throat and turned toward Angela, "Uh, Angela, there's something I'd like to . . . I need your help with, ah, something . . ."

"Sure," Angela said absently, still gazing out the window. When Kyle remained silent, she looked his way. He shifted from one foot to another and took off his glasses, polishing them on a corner of his shirt. He had really long eyelashes for a guy—she'd never noticed behind the thick glasses. "So? What do you want?" she asked.

"Uh, well, I don't *want* anything . . . I just thought you might be the right person to ask for help about this . . . uh, problem. Well, it's not really a problem—it's just a situation."

"So, tell me already!" Angela said, giving him a shove.

"Ah, well, you know I sort of got stuck with the job of Student Council reporter for the school newspaper, and so I have to go to their official functions . . . to report and all. Well, there's this one coming up, and I'm supposed to bring a friend. It's just an official thing I need to be at actually, not a date or anything . . . and I was thinking since you've written some articles for the paper, you might be the right person to ask to go with me?"

It was embarrassing to see Kyle so tongue-tied. "What exactly is this official event?" she asked suspiciously.

"Huh, yeah. Well, it's actually a dance," he admitted, then rushed to add, "but it wouldn't be a date or anything—just friends going to hear some music, probably by a really bad local band. I'm thinking it might be really boring, but if you were there we could make it fun, you know?"

Was her friend asking for a date? Unbelievable. She stared at him for a minute. His face was completely drained of color and his expression looked like he was bracing for a punch in the stomach. It was kind of endearing. Suddenly she pictured him walking into the dance all alone with this same expression on his face. She couldn't let that happen to a friend.

"Well, sure. We'd be going as friends, right?" she agreed. "I mean, that's not technically a date."

"Oh, yeah. Absolutely!" Kyle exclaimed. "It'll be fun. And totally platonic. It's two weeks from this Friday."

"Okay, no problem. I'll put it in my planner," Angela said.

Why did it seem he had been working so hard to reassure her about the non-dating status of this event? Was he trying to convince Angela or himself? What if he wanted to become more than friends? Would it ruin their relationship?

Well, she'd have to risk it now that she'd said yes and he looked so relieved. Anyway, after saying all that about it being "just friends" he'd have some serious difficulty converting it to anything more serious.

Kyle turned back to the window and scanned the view. Now that it was over he was trying to think of some way to change the subject back to something normal. His mind was blank.

Footsteps in the Dark

ARRRA! Come here! Carrra . . ."

Cara heard her mommy calling from the back door. She knew Mommy probably couldn't see her sitting behind the lavender bush. It must be time to go to bed. She hated to stop playing so soon. She crawled into the little doghouse Uncle Noel had built for Ginger and Peachy. The puggles were out in the truck with him, so their little house was empty. It was dark and warm inside. She giggled a little when she saw her mom's feet go right by the doorway. This was like hide-and-seek. Maybe she'd jump out and say "Boo!" when Mommy came by again.

Cara waited, but her mom's voice kept getting farther away. She started to crawl out of the doghouse, and the crystal jewel from her necklace snagged on a nail and bumped onto the wooden floor. Oops! She picked it up and looked at it to see if it had broken. She could see the moonlight shining through it. In the middle of the crystal there was a silver figure that looked like a little angel dancing. The crystal spun on its chain, and the angel looked like it was dancing around and around inside the walls of the crystal. The moonlight reflected from the pretty jewel and bounced around the garden path. It looked like the dancer inside the crystal. It was skipping from leaf to leaf and going down the path toward the barn. Cara jumped up and tried to touch it, but it moved farther down the path. It was getting dark, so she should go in now. She looked back over her shoulder at the house. Then she looked at the shiny angel light again. She reached out to touch it, and it ran away. She started chasing it, slowly at first, then faster and faster. The angel danced right through the barn door. It was gone. But the door opened. Cara peeked inside. The pretty silver angel stood inside the secret room. He waved to her and skipped a little. What was he holding in his hand? He had her little black horse. How did he get that? He held it out to her. She ran to get it back from him. Suddenly, she felt herself falling. It felt like the floor had turned into water and everything around her looked white.

The Chalice Moon was beginning to rise in the sky, and the last bit of sunset had almost faded. There was just enough reflected light to see Bren's bright blond hair bobbing up and down along the ridge of the pasture. He had gone out to get the horses from the far corner of the pasture and bring them inside the warm barn for the night. He was riding bareback on Bobcat and leading Sammy with Roy following them. He knew Angela would say he shouldn't ride Bobcat without a saddle and bridle if she saw him, but they were in an enclosed pasture, and Bren could tell the pony had started to trust him. Anyway, no one would be able to see him this far away from the house at dusk. The way Angela watched over him you'd think he'd never fallen from a horse before. So what if he had to pay some dues to the upsidedown club? It would be worth it to ride Bobcat. He was so sleek and fast compared with Sammy. With that fancy crystal halter band Marti had put on him, Bobcat looked like a parade horse—or an elf lord's steed! Bren watched the halter's jewels sparkle in the growing moonlight. It was almost like a headlight illuminating the path in front of them. This was exactly how an elf lord would feel riding in the twilight on an enchanted horse.

153

Swirls of fog had begun to settle near the warm ground as the night chill rolled in.

As they got near the barn, he noticed that the barn door was already open. He had left the light on, but he was sure he had closed the door. Then he saw a movement near the entrance. Who was that going inside? Somebody small. He couldn't be sure—the night mist was rising and growing thicker in front of him—but it looked like Cara. Boy, she was really going to be in trouble if she was messing around in the barn alone! She knew better than to come down there without him or Angela. And it was almost dark, too. She was probably trying to find an excuse to stay up longer. Maybe she had thought up a reason to come and see him before going to bed and had talked her dad into letting her go.

"Hey, Cara!" he called out. No response. He could no longer see her. Sammy suddenly planted his feet and wouldn't budge. Roy stopped cold, too. Bren pulled on the rope halter. "C'mon, boy," he coaxed. At the same moment, Bobcat jerked his lead rope out of Bren's hand and charged ahead to the barn door. Bren dropped Sammy's rope and hung on to Bobcat's mane. Without the lead rope to rein him in, Bobcat was in control. The pony was probably just racing to the feed bin in his stall. Bren braced himself for a quick stop inside the barn and yelled, "Watch out! Watch out! Coming through!" in case Cara was in the aisle. Bren made it through the door without losing his seat and got ready for a sliding stop. But Bobcat didn't stop. It was confusing. Where the door to the secret room should have been, there was a big open space that led to ... nothing. Bobcat gathered himself as if to go over a jump and leaped into the white space ahead with the terrified boy clinging to his back.

Bren braced himself again, expecting to feel the full impact of the ground rushing up to meet them when the pony landed. But it didn't come. One minute he was sitting on Bobcat's back and the next he was floating in space. Alone.

Everything was white around him like the white fog they had jumped into, but Bobcat was gone. Then he began to feel something hard beneath him. He was sitting on something again. The white fog began to clear and he could make out a face. Someone was bending over him and trying to talk to him. He rubbed his eyes. Some of the fog cleared. It was Marti. She was talking to him, but he couldn't understand her. Then he felt like she was pushing on his shoulders. She was telling him to lie down. Maybe he had fallen. Maybe he was hurt. He gave in and let himself relax until he could feel his head was lying on something soft. He was very cold. Marti put a gray blanket over him. It made him feel even colder, and he thought it must have been very heavy because he couldn't move his arms or legs.

Marti's words that had sounded like they were coming to him from under water became clearer. "It's okay, Bren. We just want to help you. Lie still."

There was another person with her. A boy dressed in gray with white hair and black eyes that shone from his pale face. He was saying something to Bren in a strange tone, like he was repeating a rhyme over and over, but the words didn't make any sense. Bren began to feel dizzy, and he closed his eyes.

155

30

Angel Lights

K YLE DIDN'T need to come up with a way to change the subject from the dance to something else. As they were staring out the window in awkward silence, four flashes of light shot from four of the hills, including the one they were standing on. The lights flew across the valley and met near the middle. It looked as if a shooting star had come from each hill. The light had a flicker like a shooting star would. Neither was sure if they'd actually seen anything—except that they both had seen something.

"What was that?" they both asked at the same time. Before they could answer, they heard Chloe come back inside the house, still calling for Cara. But now she was also calling Bren and Angela's mom had joined her. They came to the library and asked Angela and Kyle to help them look. "Sure," they both answered at the same time.

Angela had an idea. "We'll check the barn and the lower end of the garden. They might be saying goodnight to the horses."

"That's a good idea," Mom said. "Cara's used that excuse to stretch out bedtime deadline before. Bren's friends are supposed to come over to work on homework together, so he should be finishing up down there."

Angela had just put her hand on the knob of the outside door to open it when the doorbell rang and made her jump. She opened it and both she and Kyle were startled again. Five of Bren's ghoulfriends were lurking there on the porch in full costume.

"Ugh!" Angela greeted them, and then she said, "Follow me."

Kyle shook his head. He'd seen the group before, but this looked a little too real in the twilight. Creepy little kids. One of them had a leather drum that he was beating slowly as he walked. A couple of the others were carrying toy crossbows made from pieces of wood with large rubber bands stretched across them that could certainly hurt if a shot hit you. Kyle didn't like to have them walking behind him. He threw them a warning look, and one of them snickered.

"Uh, so what kind of homework are you guys doing?" Kyle asked.

"Ooh, we bring Bren's homework. Evil message from the witch queen," said one of the boys with an overly dramatic accent from behind his rubber mask.

"Yeah, we come to torture Bren!" slurred another ghoul and the rest of them grunted and cheered in agreement.

Angela rolled her eyes, and Kyle shrugged, "My little brother is weird, too."

As they got near the barn, they could see that the door was open and a light was coming from it. "They must be inside," Angela said. She turned to the ghoulfriends. "You stay here. I don't want you to scare my horses."

The ghouls were only too happy to hide themselves around the outside of the fence and wait to surprise their friend Bren. "Don't tell Bren we're here," the closest one hissed.

Inside the barn Angela was very surprised to find no one, no people or horses. She went back outside to look for them. Ouch! Something stung her on the arm. A rubber band landed beside her foot.

"It's just his sister," one of Bren's friends whispered from the bushes. "Sorry!"

Kyle followed her as she walked out of the barn to look for her horses and her brother. "Bren!" she called. Roy and Sammy nickered and came trotting out of the shadows. "Hey, guys," she coaxed. They came right up to her and Kyle. Now Angela was worried. Where could Bren be, and was Cara with him? And where was Bobcat? He should be tagging along with her horses. All kinds of ideas came to mind. Had Bren tried to ride the pony and fallen? Was Cara with him somewhere out there trying to help him? She ran into the barn and flipped the switch for the outside light. Then she grabbed a flashlight. She, Kyle, and the ghoulfriends searched the pasture, calling Bren. No luck. She was about to go back to the house to see if they had come home when she saw Mom and Aunt Chloe and Grandma coming down the path to the barn.

"Did you find them?" Chloe called.

"No, I was hoping you had," Angela said. "I'm scared."

Chloe and Mom looked at each other. It was obvious they were scared, too. Grandma put an arm around them. "Jesus, guide us and keep Bren and Cara safe," she said, looking up at the heavens. "Send your angels to protect them."

They all turned to look as a loud engine revved from down the road. Coming over the hill they saw a motorcycle headlight. Billy Joe Countryman slid his motorcycle to a stop when he saw the crowd at the barn. He lifted the visor on his helmet and called out to Angela, "Hey, have you heard from Marti tonight?"

"No, why?"

"What about her mom? Has she been here?" he asked.

"No. We've been out here looking for Bren and Cara," Angela said.

"Well, that makes four people missing now," Billy Joe said.

"What? What's going on?" Mom asked.

"Mr. Philips called and said both Marti and her mom were missing," Billy Joe explained. "They haven't been at the barn and when Sara told us, I decided to ride out to see if I could find her and Bobcat on any of the paths. Chuck is with Mr. Philips at their house."

"Well, she didn't have Bobcat to ride away on this time," Angela said. "He's been here since we found him in the woods last time. But *he's* missing, too."

"You know where I think we should look, don't you?" Billy Joe said to Angela. "Let's go back to that place in the woods where you found Marti last time. The story you told me about that guy with the crystals has been bugging me ever since I heard about it."

"Yeah, something's wrong with that whole story," Kyle added.

Billy Joe looked at him as if noticing Kyle for the first time. Then he turned to Angela. "Hop on back and help me find the place again. Here's an extra helmet."

"Wait, I want to come with you, too," Angela's mom said. "With Bobcat missing there's a good chance Bren is with her."

"I'll give Angela a ride, and Billy Joe can take you," Kyle offered.

Billy Joe looked startled. "Uh, sure. That's fine."

Angela grabbed a black riding helmet from the barn and ran back to the house with Kyle. "This is crazy. How could all these people be missing?"

As they reached the house and Kyle's scooter, the front door opened, and Grandpa waved them over. "Is your Grandma out there?"

"She's at the barn with Aunt Chloe. They'll be back up here in a minute." Chloe and Grandma decided to stay at the house and get Mike and Grandpa to keep looking for Bren and Cara on the property. Since no one knew for sure if the disappearances were related, they felt they should stay there and keep searching.

Grandpa looked worried and said, "We have to go to the hospital. A nurse just called and said they can't find Candace."

31

The Missing

"THAT'S TOO many coincidences in one night for me!" Kyle exclaimed.

"I agree! Grandpa, you'd better call the police. Kyle and Billy Joe and Mom and I are going back to the cottage where I found Marti. We think that strange guy she met there might have something to do with this." Angela got on the back of the scooter and Kyle started it up.

Before Grandpa could say another word, they were on their way. Billy Joe saw them coming and pulled into the road ahead of them. Kyle mumbled something Angela could barely hear. It sounded like he was unhappy to follow behind Billy Joe, but he had no choice. There was no way the red scooter could match a real motorcycle's speed, and Billy Joe was not sparing his engine tonight.

Marti's mom wasn't sure where she was now, but she felt completely at rest and, through the white fog, Lorena Philips could hear her daughter's voice saying, "Don't worry, Mom. You're going to be all right. Your happy ending is going to come true tonight."

The last thing she remembered was sitting at the dressing table in her bedroom removing her makeup. She hated to see herself without eye shadow anymore. There was a time when she had never felt the need for cosmetics. It seemed so long ago now—college days were another lifetime. She had been so pretty before she became a wife and mother. Boys called for dates and gave her "that look" when she waved to them, or when she ignored them. She hadn't seen her husband give her a look like that for some time. She had been just as pretty then as her daughter was now. Marti didn't know how lucky she was and how exciting her life was about to become. This boy, Clay, was the first one she'd shown any interest in, but it sounded like Marti thought of him as just another friend.

163

"Youth is wasted on the young," she said into the mirror. Who was that middle-aged woman staring back at her so hopelessly? "Good grief, the bags under my eyes have bags," she complained.

"You're still so beautiful," said a voice. She turned to look, but her husband wasn't home yet. And that certainly didn't sound like a comment he'd make. Not anymore. All he cared about was his career and people who could help it advance. Maybe the voice she'd heard was Marti turning on the TV from the other bedroom. She looked back in the mirror. Maybe she should have some work done. There was a new spa in Rocky River that was supposed to perform miracles on wrinkles. Lorena pulled her face back at the sides and thought how she'd look with a lift. Yes, she needed a miracle . . .

"Your inner beauty just needs to open up," said the voice again. This time she could see a silhouette in the background of her mirror. She turned around to look behind her, but no one was there. When she turned back to the mirror, she gasped. Her reflection had been transformed. It looked the way she always pictured herself in her mind—young and beautiful—until she caught her reflection somewhere and her worry wrinkles reminded her that those days were behind her.

"You've been disappointed in your life, but that is about to change," came the voice from the mist behind her reflection. "It wasn't fair. He promised to make you his princess, not his maid or his child's nanny. You've wasted your life waiting for Prince Charming to come home late and eat leftovers with you. It isn't fair," said the voice as a sculpted face began to appear from the mist. "You deserve a real prince." The young man looked like an angel made of light. Lorena couldn't take her eyes off him. She must be dreaming. But his dark eyes had that look she had been missing for so long. That look of admiration and desire. His hand reached toward her, and she automatically extended her hand in return. She was startled when she felt the touch of his fingertips on hers, and the mist from the mirror became part of her room. It swirled around her, then fell across her shoulders like a cape—but instead of feeling warm, it felt chill. She became so sleepy that she decided to lie down. Then she forgot where she had been or why she was so unhappy before.

At the high school across town, Teri Gibson was putting away her saxophone in the band room lockers. It had been a great practice. Simone had been drunk with power on her first day as section leader, but reality soon brought her back down to earth. Simone was so diligent about her music that all it took was one wrong note to humble her and send her scurrying to a practice booth to work on scales. Teri wished she could find such a satisfying remedy for the sour notes in her own life. She was probably headed for a restless night of insomnia or awful dreams because her history teacher had assigned an especially disturbing reading for tonight. An expert compared the causes of the first two world wars so he could project how long it would take for another global conflict to happen. Teri would have to finish reading it before going to bed, so she'd be ready for a quiz first period tomorrow. She was already replaying the lecture over and over in her mind.

165

"Those who don't learn from history are doomed to repeat it," her teacher had warned. Teri looked around the empty band room and hurried to finish up. The place looked eerie with most of the lights off and the moonlight streaming in through the windows. Her locker door echoed loudly as she threw it shut. The word *doomed* beat a rhythm in her brain. Everything was starting to look and sound funny. She was probably coming down with a migraine. Yep. There were the halos forming around the edges of her vision like heat waves on asphalt. Next they'd start to turn into rainbows and signal a full-blown headache. She shook a migraine pill from the bottle in her purse. Sometimes the pills would stop the process if she took them soon enough. It slid down her throat with a couple of gulps from the fountain by the lockers. That water was freezing, and she shivered. She must have stood up too quickly, she thought, because everything suddenly began to spin. It felt like the wall had turned to cotton candy when she put out her hand to brace herself on it. *Omigosh, I'm fainting*, she thought as she felt herself falling. Everything became white cotton candy mist, and she braced herself for the impact of hitting the floor. It never came.

Simone, Michelle, and Adam came into the band room to put their instruments in the lockers just in time to see Teri start to faint. But she didn't slump to the floor as they expected. She seemed to melt into the wall and disappear!

Clay opened his arms and caught Teri as she fell into the cottage through the west wall. Her long hair streamed over his arm, and crumpled into a heap of gold locks on top of a gray pillow as he lowered her to the floor and smiled into her lovely, sleeping face. The crystal on the necklace Marti had given her glowed with milky light on the front of her pink sweater. Clay covered her with a gray blanket. "Our last voyager," he said to Marti. "Safe and sound."

"Is she really okay?" Marti asked nervously. Teri didn't look right in the misty light. Her rosy complexion had faded to white. Her breathing was so shallow that Marti could barely see it. Candace had looked the same way when she entered the room, and Marti glanced over at her sleeping form lying against the north wall.

"Yes, she and Candace were the easiest to bring through The Lines and help into a dreaming state because they had taken potions before their voyage," the boy explained serenely.

"What potions? You mean medicine?" Marti asked, guessing Clay was using another old-fashioned term for something. It was funny that this guy her own age sometimes threw in words that only a very old person or a character in an old book might use.

"Yes, that's right. And now that they are all here together the strength of their dreams and wishes will be enough to make them all come true. Theirs and yours," he said, taking her hands in his.

32

The Lines

Yes," MARTI said faintly, looking into his dark eyes. They were like a midnight sky with tiny flecks of stars that appeared when you looked into them deeply. Their gaze was so calming. She began to have that same floating feeling she had experienced when Clay took her "for a ride" on his private transport system that he called "The Lines." They had "voyaged," as he called it, from the cottage to Angela's barn in seconds the other day.

The three horses had tried to kick the barn down when Clay appeared in the secret room, so he had left her there to visit Bobcat alone and put the crystal head-stall on his halter. With it Bobcat would be able to travel from point-to-point on The Lines as she and Clay had done. He explained that each Line began and ended near an old cornerstone on one of the hills in the Emerald

Circle, like a chain connecting jewels on a necklace, he had told her. You could open a Line from almost any room in whatever building had been built over the ancient stone. All the cornerstones also had Lines that were connected to the one under the cottage, like spokes on a wheel. Clay said they had existed as long as people had lived there, even though many different buildings had stood above them.

"The knowledge of The Lines and how to travel using them was passed down to me from my people," he explained. Marti guessed he meant his family. He said they were supposed to guard The Lines from anyone who tried to use them without permission. Whenever the stars in the Big Dipper lined up with the necklace, The Lines could be traveled.

"But," he warned, "whenever there is a red color on the moon, voyagers on The Lines could meet great danger unless they have a crystal. The red color signals that an attack on The Lines is coming."

When Marti asked who was attacking, Clay had said it was "outside powers" and that he couldn't explain in a way she'd understand. "But we are the true princes of this world," he said so seriously that she didn't doubt him.

She had never met royalty before, but Marti imagined that they must be like Clay, very certain of their ancient right and so mysterious. *Maybe it has something to do with Native American royalty*, she thought, but Clay didn't seem to know what she meant when she asked him.

Whatever technical explanation Clay had for all this, Marti was satisfied to understand that her wishes were coming true and her troubles were going to be solved. To begin with, she would be able to hide her horse at the cottage and ride him whenever she wanted. Clay had promised to make sure no one would ever know. The crystal band had an immediate calming effect on Bobcat, though it had seemed to Marti that Sammy must have been jealous when he tried to take the pretty thing from her hand as she was putting it on her pony. Once Bobcat was wearing his flashy jewelry, he kept it safe. He would not let Sammy near it. Marti had been ready to test it and take Bobcat through the Line that led from Angela's barn to the cottage when her friend had opened the barn door and surprised her.

After Clay had given her a great gift and was about to do even more for her, he asked for her trust. "I need your help to defend The Lines from the Powers when they attack it. It would be too strong for you and me to defeat alone, but if you could convince some others to believe in the crystal, we would win the battle together. And we could help your friends at the same time if they will come to the cottage."

Marti couldn't think how she would get anyone to come. Especially Angela. She didn't want to believe in the crystals, Marti told him.

"Just give her one to wear. We'll take her for a ride on The Lines and prove it to her," Clay grinned. So he thought Angela's surprise voyage had been set in place that night. He was the one to be surprised when he saw Cara coming to the barn wearing the necklace instead of Angela. Marti thought Clay might be upset with her for the mistake, but the boy had gently touched Cara's forehead, then commented quietly, "She'll do."

He laid the sleeping child on a pillow by the south wall where she had come through and covered her with one of his silvery gray blankets. They were made of some kind of reflective material that was light as a cobweb, but very strong. Marti had no idea how strong it was until Bobcat came leaping through the translucent wall with Bren on board. He jumped over the sleeping Cara and halted just outside the doorway on the porch. Clay had been taken by surprise, but he quickly caught a falling Bren in one of the blankets as if in a net. He wrapped Bren up in it and the blanket held as firmly against his semi-conscious struggles as a bundle of rope.

"He wasn't properly protected for a voyage," Clay explained after Bren fell into a fitful sleep. "It's very dangerous to jump into an open line without the protection of a crystal of your own, especially during a red moon. He should be all right after a while, but I'm afraid he will have some strange dreams until this is over."

Marti thought it looked like Bren was dreaming something troubling. His eyes moved back and forth rapidly under their almost-closed lids, and he exhaled little puffs of breath as if he were trying to speak.

"Maybe we should send him back," Marti said nervously. "We weren't expecting him, and this is a small space. We don't need extra people, right?" She looked around the little cottage. Her mother was lying on the floor by the east wall. Teri's sleeping figure stretched out along the west wall, and Angela's aunt Candace was across the room by the north wall.

Clay put his hand on Bren's forehead. "This one has a lot of desires that haven't been fulfilled. He belongs here. He can attend the door." Marti led Bobcat down into the yard, and he hopped obediently over the porch steps, landing in front of the little house. Clay followed after, laying Bren across the threshold of the doorway. He looked at Bobcat, who now seemed unafraid of him. "Guard this place," Clay commanded. Bobcat turned slowly around to face the path and planted his feet squarely in the sod. He was so still that he looked as if he had been turned into an ebony statue of a horse, like the model horse Clay had placed on the floor next to the sleeping Cara.

"Now it is time to set our defense in place and bring our wishes to fulfillment," Clay said, letting go of Marti's hands and walking around the room. He held a hand over Candace's head and spoke in a language Marti didn't understand. Then he ended in English words, "All your doubt and loneliness will be ended this night." He walked to Teri and said the foreign words, again before adding, "Your questions will all be answered and your fear ended this night." He stood by Bren and ended his words by saying, "Your desires will be fulfilled this night, and you will want no more." He walked to Cara, and the last words he spoke were, "You will not have to leave your joyous game again." He stood over Lorena Philips last and Marti watched him lift her mom's hand and kiss it tenderly before he said, "And you will be beautiful forever and never mourn your youth again."

Clay turned back to Marti and took her hands again. "Are you ready to do your part?"

She nodded and the room became filled with bluish light. It seemed to be coming in streams from the bodies of the sleeping people as if they were pointing flashlights at Marti and Clay. Then Marti realized that she and Clay were both floating several inches above the floor. "You and I are the center of this defense just as the stone in this place is the center of The Lines. Whatever happens, look only into my eyes. Then we will be strong and you will not be afraid." They began turning slowly in a circle as they floated, hand-in-hand in the middle of the strange light and her sleeping friends.

173

33

The Battle Begins

ANGELA HELD tightly to Kyle's waist as they left the road and bumped along the trail. Her dad should be getting home soon. Boy, would he be coming into the middle of a wild story! She was sure Grandma and Grandpa had left for the hospital as soon as they could get into the car. Mike and Chloe would be holding down the home front with Dad if any news of Cara or Bren came there. But on some completely intuitive level, Angela felt that the children were with Marti and Bobcat at the old cottage. What they would find there was beyond anything she imagined, however.

As they came over the hill, Billy Joe's headlight revealed a strange sight on the path ahead—Bobcat standing in the path to the house with his head down as if to charge the vehicles like a bull. His eyes glowed red in the headlight—or were they red without the headlight? Billy Joe tried to swerve off the path to go around the horse, but Bobcat moved to block them, bared his teeth, and began screaming in a way that didn't sound like any domestic animal Angela had ever heard. It was somewhere between a horse's challenge squeal and a lion's roar.

Kyle braked hard, bringing his bike to a stop behind Billy Joe. Bobcat stood in their way pawing the ground and making it clear he wasn't going to let them pass, but he didn't charge. Billy Joe turned his bike around and let Angela's mom get off. "Good thing I always carry a rope in case of emergency," Billy Joe said grimly. He opened the saddlebag on his bike and pulled out a lasso. "That horse has gone crazy. I'm only going to get one shot at this, so be ready to break through to the cottage as soon as I get the rope around his neck. I don't think he's stronger than the two hundred horses I've got in this baby, but we'll see."

Billy Joe charged back down the hill and turned off the path as if he were going away. Bobcat watched him go, then turned to face Kyle's bike to see if it would go away as well. While Bobcat was distracted, Billy Joe circled back and headed toward him from the side. Before the horse could turn to face him, Billy Joe threw his lasso. It arched perfectly through the air, over Bobcat's head, and came to rest around the pony's neck. He drove the bike in a circle that would loop his end of the rope around a nearby tree, so he could use it for leverage and a hitching post. What he had counted on was that Bobcat

175

would resist him, but the horse decided to charge him instead. Billy Joe looked back in terror at the red-eyed demon horse chasing his motorcycle. It was going to be really hard to get the rope around the tree if the horse followed him. What he needed was another roper to throw a lasso around the horse and pull him to a stop from the opposite direction. Suddenly, he got his wish. A lasso snaked through the air and stopped the pony before his bared teeth could take a chunk out of Billy Joe's jeans. Angela's dad had broken through the woods on Roy Rogers, and he had not forgotten how to throw a rope.

"Hallelujah!" shouted Billy Joe as the pony stopped short, held between the two ropes like a crosstie.

As soon as the word came from Billy Joe's mouth, a strange thing happened. Bobcat dropped to his knees as if he had been shot. He stayed there as if frozen. It looked like he was bowing to the men.

They didn't have time to do more about Bobcat than to tie him to the tree. He wasn't going anywhere and Angela's mom was shouting, "Bren! It's Bren! Help!" while she sprinted toward the cottage doorway. Kyle and Angela kept up with her on the bike, then jumped off and left it at the edge of the porch.

At first, they all stood on the porch staring at the strange scene. They had certainly never seen anyone levitate before and they stared at Marti and Clay floating in the center of the room. Eerie bluish lights radiated from Bren's body as it blocked the doorway and they could see other lights coming from bodies lying across the room.

Angela's mom had just reached the doorway and dropped to her knees beside Bren, but she stopped herself from gathering up her son in her arms when she heard the stranger's warning.

"These humans are my hostages," said Clay in a hollow, echoing voice. "If you touch them, they will die."

"Wait!" said Dad as he caught up to them. "Don't touch him! Bobcat was released from his spell when Billy Joe shouted a word of praise to God. I have an idea."

And Dad did something completely unexpected. He began to sing, "Glory be to the Father, and to the Son, and to the Holy Ghost . . ."

Mom joined in, and they sang the rest together, "As it was in the beginning, is now, and ever shall be, world without end. A-men. A-men."

177

The light began to fade from Bren, and his breath came in gasps. He coughed and opened his eyes. "C'mon," Dad called to the others, "Everyone sing." They started the holy song over. Angela knew it by heart from church. It was called the "Gloria Patri," a hymn of praise they sometimes ended a church service by singing. She had never thought of using it anywhere else.

Bren turned and looked at his family. "Help!" he called weakly.

"Sing, Bren," Mom urged him. "Sing with us."

The little boy began faintly, and slowly his voice grew stronger. As it did, he sat up and threw off the blanket that had bound his arms and legs. It melted away into shreds as if it were really just made of cobwebs after all.

"No, no," shrieked Clay. "You are calling them! Stop it! You will bring the enemies down on this place!" He was still holding Marti by the hands, staring into her unblinking eyes, and turning slowly as they floated.

"Keep singing!" yelled Dad. "It's working!"

So they did it. And as they sang, Marti and Clay slowly stopped turning and inched back toward the floor. Gradually, they began to hear other voices joining their song from inside the cottage.

The first to come outside was Aunt Candace, helping Teri walk. Both of them dusted cobwebs from their clothes as they sang the "Gloria Patri." The silver necklaces had turned black and were falling apart like old straw, along with the crystals that now looked like broken cocoons that some moth had left behind.

"Look," Candace said when they were at the door. She pointed to the wall where she had lain and there was a bright light coming from it. Through what looked like a window with frosted glass, they could see Grandma and Grandpop. Then they heard their voices singing the "Gloria Patri." They looked over at the wall where Teri had been and saw Simone, Michelle, and Adam. They heard them singing, too.

"Get out of there, Teri," they heard Adam call. Then they saw Simone pick up her saxophone. She started to play the melody they'd been singing loudly. The other sax players did the same. A powerful vibration made the little building tremble as soon as they did so.

"They must be able to see us and hear us," said Teri.

34

The Stairway

MARTI TURNED her eyes away from Clay and looked at her mom. Clay suddenly lost his footing and dropped Marti's hands to catch himself he fell to the ground. "No, no, look at me! Take my nds!" he yelled, clawing at the air as he went down. His ooth voice rose to a screech and his serene face was torted with fear. For a few seconds, Marti looked at n writhing on the floor, then she ran to her mom and gged her.

"You are a bad angel," accused a small voice from de the room.

"Cara!" Angela called out when she saw her cousin king toward the doorway.

"He took my horse," Cara said, pointing at Clay. 's a bad angel. The good angel said so."

"Keep singing," yelled Dad again. They all d

Suddenly the wall by Marti's mom began
On the other side of the frosted window, they say
Countryman and Marti's dad. Both men were sir
"Gloria Patri."

"Lorena," called Mr. Philips. "I love you. I
Come back to me."

Mrs. Philips sat up. When she saw her hu
began to weep. Chuck had his arm around Mr
keep him from trying to come through the wi
Philips touched the glasslike window, then qu
her hand away as if burned by its coldness.

"Come here, Lorena," called Angela's m
think you can go back that way—it's danger
come to you. We'll take you home to him."

Marti's mom stood up and started walki
cottage. Then she saw her daughter. She ar
standing on the floor, but still holding hands
ing at me, Marti," begged Clay. "Help m
away."

"Marti!" called her mom.

Cara was leading someone by the hand. It wasn't anyone they knew, and it didn't look like anyone they'd ever seen before, except maybe in a Bible illustration.

"Now that's what I call an angel," said Billy Joe, taking off his helmet.

"I was called to come help you over a week ago," said the beautiful golden creature holding Cara's hand. "By you and you and you . . ." he said, pointing to Angela first, then her mom, then Aunt Candace. "But I couldn't get through because the Prince of the Emerald Circle was resisting me." He gestured with his open hand in Clay's direction. The difference between the two was striking. The light coming from Cara's angel was warm as the sun, and next to its brilliance, Clay's glow looked cold and deathly. The angel's face seemed to embody wisdom and love, while Clay's expression had turned to hatred and deceit. "He had convinced some of you to aid him, and I could not battle him or he would injure his hostages."

"He used us as hostages?" cried Marti. "He said he was going to make our dreams come true!" Clay's eyes blinked rapidly, and he covered his face as if this truth and the angel's light were inflicting pain.

The angel's face became sad when he said, "I am sorry for what he has done to you. He is a liar, like the leader of his kind. If he had continued to take your strength and that of your friends to shield this place, you would have been lost and the fulfillment of your wishes only an illusion as you faded from life."

181

"What kind of creature is he?" Angela shuddered as she looked at Clay cowering before them.

"He used to be my kind." The angel looked at them with what seemed to be embarrassment as he answered. "He is one of the fallen."

"How did he get this power over us?" asked Bren. "Was it the crystals?"

"Neither he nor the crystals could have any power over you without your consent," the angel said looking around at each one slowly. "Nor can I! You are your own masters unless you give your hearts to another. Unless you let fear or doubt or envy master you."

A tear fell down Marti's face, and she shook her head very sadly. "I just wanted my family to stay together. What will happen to us now?"

The angel turned to the girl, and there seemed to be a mist of gold that rained from his outstretched hands toward her. "You are right to desire this," he said. "But it is not your decision to make alone. You must have patience, and hope for wisdom and healing to prevail. You are young and this is a difficult task, but you will grow wise yourself from all that you experience, no matter what happens."

"What about The Lines?" she asked. "Can people really travel them with crystals?"

The angel smiled mysteriously, "The crystals were part of this one's deception, but you may learn more about the Angel Lines in time. They are not to be used lightly. In times past there were faithful souls who learned how to

escape great danger and great evil by traveling them—
with my help. Before them an ancient people came
together from far places to worship the one, true God
here. But they did not have cars, motorcycles, or airplanes
to travel in. What need do you have to use The Lines?"

"It's just so cool!" Bren exclaimed.

The angel laughed a little, and showers of gold rain-
drops danced from his hair. "It is just a small thing in a
universe so large. Your life seems far more 'cool' to us than
the dusty old machinery of angels."

"What should we do about this place and about
him?" asked Angela pointing to Clay, who shuddered and
winced.

The angel frowned and said, "He holds the key to
this place—that is why he named himself Clé— but you
believers have the keys to the Kingdom. Will you take his
key as well?"

"How?" asked Angela.

"It is yours by right. All you need to do is ask for it,"
the angel replied.

"Give us that key," commanded Billy Joe, stepping
forward. "And you hit the road and leave Marti alone.
Don't ever come back here to bother her. I'm telling you
as a believer in the name of Jesus."

Clay jerked away, scrambling on the floor, and
screamed a long, shrill wail. Billy Joe took another step
toward him, holding out his hand for the key.

"N-o-o-o!" cried Clay as he jumped through the
only open window where you couldn't see a person

183

singing the "Gloria Patri." It was the one that led to the Clarkson's barn. As he jumped through it, a small silver key fell to the ground. Billy Joe picked it up.

"What are we supposed to do with it?" he asked the angel.

"If you want my wisdom, I would say you should lock up this place for now," the angel answered. "If you command me to guard it; I will," he offered. "Then I can more easily come when you call upon God for help."

Billy Joe looked around at everyone. "That sounds like an offer we shouldn't refuse," advised Dad.

Billy Joe handed the key to the golden figure who then walked over to the window Clay had taken and put the key into the middle of it. As the window shrank into nothing, they caught a glimpse of a white hand that seemed to be beating on a misty wall of glass as if wanting to come through. The other windows faded one by one as well.

184

"I think that one was trying to change his mind," the angel smiled. Then he lifted his hands the way pastors do after everyone finishes singing and said, "But the rest of you seem to have made up your minds and hearts. You have chosen the blessed way, and from now on this place will be filled with your peace. My brethren and I will visit you in season and bless your land."

With that the angel began walking as if he were climbing a stairway. And he kept climbing that way until he was too far into the sky for them to see him any longer. The Chalice Moon seemed to have emptied its wine and the Big Dipper twinkled next to it. Bobcat and the horses grazed on the grass under the stars as if nothing out of the ordinary had happened to them. The friends sat on the ground or on the porch for a few minutes and stared after the angel, then they looked at each other and could find no words to say about what they'd just experienced.

35

The Path Home

WELL, I GUESS we'd better get home and let everyone know we're okay," Dad finally said, then began to count how many vehicles they had for the number of people. If Marti and Angela rode double on Roy, he could lead Cara and Bren back home on Bobcat. Aunt Candace could ride with Billy Joe, and Mom with Kyle. But that still left Teri and Mrs. Philips without a ride. Just then they heard the sound of a motorcycle coming over the hill. It was Mr. Philips riding Chuck's motorcycle with Chuck following behind riding Pumpkin.

Mr. Philips didn't say much. He just hugged his wife and looked at her like he was seeing her clearly for the first time in a long time—because he was.

Marti noticed this and she whispered to Angela, "You know I think I get the difference between praying for an answer and wishing for one now. Maybe I just needed to ask God to take care of my parents instead of trying to make things work out by my own power."

"Yeah, that's true. Prayer is different than wishing. It's not about getting what you want when you want it," Angela said as she slowly realized more of her questions were being answered. "I think it's about giving your problems to God and trusting the answer he brings."

Dad was still working out the transportation for everyone. "Chuck, it looks like we have a ride for everyone except Teri. Would you mind taking her with you on your horse?"

Chuck helped Teri onto Pumpkin. "I've never ridden before," she said, blushing for some reason. Why did this cowboy look a lot like a knight in shining armor to her?

"Don't worry about a thing," Chuck said, vaulting up behind her on the saddle-less horse. "Pumpkin won't let us fall."

As the two rode away together, Kyle and Angela threw each other a did-you-see-that look. Angela could tell Kyle was already coming up with a story about this in his head to tell at lunch tomorrow.

Aunt Candace said she'd be just fine to get a motorcycle ride with Billy Joe. "I've done all the resting I want for a long time. I'm not going to let fear of illness keep me in the hospital. I defeated cancer with God's help long ago. I'm healed and I'm going to live like it," she declared as she climbed on back.

Angela nodded. There were a lot of things running through her mind about what she'd seen and heard there. It seemed to confirm her deepest sense about what God is really like. She thought that maybe the answers she'd been seeking were already written on her heart; that God had been talking to her in ways she could not understand until she believed. Maybe the answer wasn't a thing, a string of words, or a formula, but a person.

The night seemed like a friendly place to ride along with the stars twinkling overhead and a "normal" crescent moon shining on their path. She looked behind her and saw Dad leading the sleepy black pony, whose sparkly crystal band had turned to dust and fallen away like the necklaces. Cara chattered as she rode along in front of Bren, enjoying being outside after dark and being up past bedtime with no complaints from her grandparents. When they got back home, Chloe and Mike were waiting outside to gather their daughter into the biggest hug ever. Cara didn't seem to mind all the attention and, for once, she was tired enough to go to bed without stalling.

Marti and Angela put their tired horses away in the barn. Sammy was already inside his stall chewing on some hay and welcomed them all with a little snort that sounded like "Humph."

Angela laughed, "About time we got here, huh, Sammy?" She rubbed his head a minute. *Poor old guy missed out on all the excitement*, she thought. Little did she know . . .

She and Marti closed up the barn and turned out the lights. Billy Joe was waiting outside, slouching on his motorcycle.

"What a night, huh? I left your Aunt Candace at the house. She seems like she's fine now. I think she enjoyed the ride!" he told the girls.

"Thanks for all your help, Billy Joe," Marti said sincerely.

"Yeah, you can really throw a rope," Angela said.

Billy Joe didn't get all puffed up from the compliment, but humbly turned to Marti with a question. "Well, I need to be getting home myself now. Do you need a ride home, Marti?"

"Hey, that's a good idea," she answered. "It'll save my parents a trip to pick me up."

189

Angela's mouth fell open, but she shut it before anyone noticed. Could this night bring any more surprises than it had already?

"Thanks, Angela. For everything!" Marti hugged her friend and took the helmet Billy Joe offered her.

What next? thought Angela as she watched them ride off.

A police patrol car was parked in their driveway and a confused officer leaned against it, holding a pen over a clipboard and shaking his head as he scribbled some notes. Angela felt sorry for the man trying to write up a report from her parents' and grandparents' description of everything that had happened.

Kyle was waiting by the door to the farmhouse. He'd gotten his book bag from the library room and was ready to go. "See you at school tomorrow?" he asked Angela.

"Sure," she said. "I guess there isn't a reason for me to stay home anymore. Good thing I finished all those worksheets before you got here."

"Yeah, well, I'll take them in with me just in case you need to sleep late or something," he said. "I think you'd be justified in taking a day to rest after all this."

"And let you be the one to tell the lunch table about Chuck and Teri? No way! See you tomorrow," she laughed and gave him a hug.

Kyle didn't have anything to say about that. He straightened his glasses and got on his minibike. "See you!" he said and sped down the drive.

Angela watched her friend go. "Hmmm," was all she said about that.

Grandma Heather and Grandpop had already arrived back at the farmhouse from the hospital. They had a lot of questions about what they had seen and heard through the strange window in Candace's empty hospital room. Grandma told Angela she had messages from Simone, Michelle, and Adam. They wanted to know if she'd come home yet, and they had a lot of questions, too!

In the farmhouse kitchen, Bren found his ghoul-friends sitting around the table finishing off the rest of Chloe's cookies while they waited for their parents to pick them up. As a group, they jumped up with a shout, tripping over each other and spilling crumbs, homework papers, and rubber bands all around the nook.

"Oh, Bren, you missed it, bud!" One of the guys started telling their story, and the others tried to add their own details to it at the same time.

"It was so cool," one began.

And another added, "We were waiting to ambush you."

"Yeah, outside the barn, man. We had a whole bag full of rubber bands and some water balloons. It was cool."

"Boy, you were going to get it. But this other guy came out instead, so we got him!"

"Yeah, we got him good. What a geek! He was so scared."

"Your pony even attacked him with us!"

"Sammy came up behind us and charged that guy like a bull!"

"Yeah, like the guy turned all white and was screaming."

"Yeah, like this 'Argh, don't take me to hell. Let me go. Eeeeek.' You know, he was totally scared."

"Yeah, like he thought we were demons going to take him to hell or something!"

"And he ran back in the barn, and we looked for him, but he was gone. He just disappeared!"

"That guy was scared good, man."

"It was so cool."

Dear Reader,

This book is just the beginning of the story about Angela and her friends and their discovery of the Angel Lines. Watch for more titles at your local bookstore or at AMG Publishing online at www.amgpublishers.com.

Read Angela's clue notebook, get free downloads, ask questions, or give your advice about her next mystery online at:

www.AngelClues.com

Look for Book Two in the **Angel Light**™
series of novels by Pat Matuszak

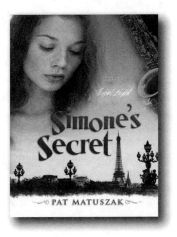

Simone is part of Angela's group of friends in *Angela's Answer*,
and she discovers the Angel Lines along with the rest of the group.
However, Simone has a secret of her own that none of her friends
suspect. They think her mother is in Paris on business, but
Simone knows she has disappeared under mysterious circum-
stances. Simone thinks she may know of a way to find her mom
and tries to complete a dangerous rescue mission alone. That's
when she finds out that she has angel helpers watching over her
who are more than willing to join her quest. They lead her across
the world to fascinating places in France, where she finds a more
amazing adventure than she ever imagined—one that will reveal
secrets about the Angel Lines and the reason for the angel wars.

AVAILABLE JULY 2008